the Wooden Ox

the Wooden Ox

LeAnne Hardy

Kregel
Publications

The Wooden Ox: A Novel

© 2002 by LeAnne Hardy

Published by Kregel Publications, P.O. Box 2607, Grand Rapids, MI 49501.

For more information about Kregel Publications, visit our Web site: www.kregel.com.

Cover design: John M. Lucas

Library of Congress Cataloging-in-Publication Data
Hardy, LeAnne.
   The wooden ox: a novel / by LeAnne Hardy
      p.   cm.
Summary: Thirteen-year-old Keri questions whether God cares when she, her younger brother, and their parents are kidnapped while doing missionary work in Mozambique and forced to walk each night farther into rebel territory.
   1. Mozambique—History—Independence and Civil War, 1975–1994—Juvenile fiction. [1. Mozambique—History—Independence and Civil War, 1975–1994—Fiction. 2. Missionaries—Fiction. 3.Guerrillas—Fiction. 4. War—Fiction. 5. Christian life—Fiction.] I. Title.
PZ7.H22143 Wo 2002
[Fic]—dc21
2002005392

ISBN   0-8254-2794-0

Printed in the United States of America

02 03 04 05 06 / 5 4 3 2 1

For Katie.
May your life be
an adventure in faith.

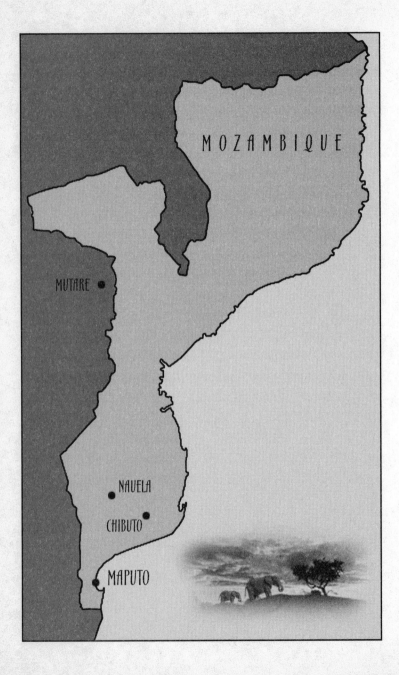

MOZAMBIQUE

MUTARE

NAUELA

CHIBUTO

MAPUTO

GLOSSARY OF NON-ENGLISH
WORDS AND PRONUNCIATION GUIDE

anda [UHN-duh] walk, get going

bem feito [bayn FAY-too] well done

bom dia [bone DEE-ah] good day

Bom Kidi [bone KEE-dee] a Mozambican game played by flicking stones or grains of corn toward a circle. The one to reach the circle in the fewest turns keeps everyone else's playing piece.

'brigada [bree-GAH-duh] short form of "thank you"

capulana [cah-poo-LAH-nuh] a piece of cloth 60 by 43 inches that is traditionally wrapped as a skirt. It has many other uses such as bed sheet or baby carrier. It usually has a bold pattern in bright colors.

claro [CLAH-roo] of course

coluna [coh-LOO-nuh] column, the name given a military convoy

com liçensa [cone lee-SAYN-sah] with your permission

comida [coh-MEE-duh] food

Dube [DOO-bay]

Dzumisana [dzoo-mee-SAH-nah] let us praise

faz nenê [fahz nay-NAY] make a baby

já [zhah] already

Jozé [zhoh-ZE]

Leila [LAYEE-luh]

Makusa [mah-KOO-suh]

Mamani [ma-MAH-nee] mother, Shangan title of respect

Mbuluzi [mm-boo-LOO-zee]

Mfana [mm-FAH-nuh] boy

mulungo [moo-LUN-goo] white man

Mutare [moo-TAH-ree]

não chore [nuhoo SHO-ree] don't cry

Nauela [nahoo-EE-luh]

Ndima [nn-DEE-muh]

nenê [nay-NAY] baby

O banho está pronto. [oo BUN-yoo es-TAH PRON-too] The
  bath is ready.

O que é? [oo key EH?] What is it?

O senhor é o meu pastor. [oo say-NYOR e oo MAYoo pah-
  STOR] The Lord is my shepherd.

obrigada, obrigado [oh-bree-GAH-duh, oh-bree-GAH-doo]
  thank you (the form depends on whether the speaker
  is female or male)

olá [oh-LAH] hello

Que é isso? [key eh EE-soo?] What's this?

rondavel [RON-da-vuhl] round traditional-style house

Rute [ROO-tee]

sei lá. [SAY LAH] Who knows.

Senhor Comandante [say-NYOR co-mahn-DAHN-tee] title
    of respect for the commander
Tomé [toh-MEH]
um momento [oon moh-MEN-too] one moment
Vamos [VUH-moos] Let's go
veld [felt] Afrikaans word for field or bush country
velho [VEH-lyoo] old man
vem cá [vayn KAH] come here
voortrekker [FOR-trek-ker] Afrikaans migrating farmer
vovô [voh-VOH] grandfather
Zulu [ZOO-loo] the strongest tribe in southeastern Africa

the Wooden Ox

CHAPTER 1

"Ow!" Keri rubbed the top of her blonde head where the springy seat had thrown her painfully against the Land Rover's ceiling. Every muscle in her long, skinny body ached from hours of jolting over the gravel road.

"Do it again, Dad!" Seven-year-old Kurt bounced on the seat beside her.

"Please don't!" Mom gave a tight laugh and gripped the dashboard.

The Andersons had been up before dawn to meet the *coluna*, as Mozambicans called the military convoy to Gaza Province. The column of cars and trucks racing across the African countryside stretched as far as Keri could see ahead and behind them. From time to time, they passed a burned-out vehicle at the side of the road—a reminder of what could happen if the Andersons pulled out of line. The *coluna* wouldn't wait while you changed a tire or a fan belt. No one traveled in this part of the country without the *coluna* since the war had spread this far south.

There was not a herdboy in sight nor a sign of a cow or

goat. Telephone lines hung in loose strands from poles leaning at odd angles.

"Look, an orange grove!" Keri said.

"Where?" Kurt demanded.

Keri pointed, but even as she did, she realized this wasn't like any orange grove she had ever seen before. Weeds choked the orderly rows. Heavy branches drooped to the ground, and the smell of rotten fruit filled the air.

"There's the farm house," Kurt said as a dark tile roof came into view. His voice faltered with uncertainty.

Keri put her head out the window as they passed and stared back at the building until it disappeared from sight. Most of the roofing was gone, and sunlight poured into deep pink and blue rooms. All the windows and doors had been taken out, leaving jagged holes where even the frames had been hammered away. The walls were scarred with little holes like chicken pox. No one needed to tell Keri they had come from gunfire.

She pulled her head into the car and stared at the back of the seat in front of her. No one said anything. *If I don't talk about it, I won't be afraid*, Keri thought. She crossed her arms and pressed them into her stomach. Dad kept his eyes on the road. Mom sat straight. She was as still as the jostling car would allow. *They aren't afraid*, Keri told herself, *and I'm not afraid either.* Kurt stared at her with eyes as big as mangos. Keri rubbed her nose to brush away the tingle of rotting oranges.

"Not much farther now." Dad broke the silence. "We're almost to the Limpopo River."

The cloud of dust ahead thickened, and the brake lights of the yellow Peugeot in front of them flashed a sudden alert. Dad braked quickly as the *coluna* lurched to a halt at the side of the road. Dust rolled in from behind.

"Close your windows!" Mom ordered, and everyone jumped to obey.

The trucks and jeeps of their escort whipped out of line and careened by. Kurt jerked back when whirling tires spattered pebbles against the glass. A truck swayed past, soldiers clinging to its sides. Most of them looked only a little older than Keri's thirteen years. She wondered if they were afraid.

As the last military vehicle passed, the driver of the yellow Peugeot turned off his car's motor. Dad did the same. In the sudden quiet, they heard the sounds of gunfire.

Keri sat very still. She could taste the dust that had seeped through the window cracks. It tickled her nostrils. Kurt sneezed. Mom fished a handkerchief from the pocket of her denim skirt and handed it to him.

"Please, don't wipe your nose on your arm," she insisted.

As if staying clean matters at a time like this. Keri chewed the nail on her left index finger and slowly exhaled. The heat and stillness of the closed car pressed in on her.

"What if the armed bandits come while the soldiers are all gone?" Kurt asked. The rebel faction in the Mozambican civil war had an official name, but where the Andersons lived in Maputo, people thought they acted more like armed bandits. Kurt's eyes were wide. His fingers gripped the back of Mom's seat until they turned white.

"The bandits are up ahead." Dad's voice was calm, but he didn't move his eyes from the direction of the shooting. Both his hands gripped the steering wheel, his knuckles as pale as Kurt's. "That's where the soldiers are going. I think we surprised them. They won't come here."

Keri hoped he was right. She didn't want to think about what could happen if he was wrong.

Slowly the dust began to settle, leaving the windshield coated with an orange film. Dad turned on the wipers to brush some of it away.

A cluster of traditional huts spilled over the top of a hill a few hundred yards ahead. Their mud walls and conical grass roofs blended with the dry ground. A flock of frantic chickens flew over a thornbush hedge, squawking noisily. A river of people streamed down the hillside. Most of them carried nothing except a child or the hoe or mallet with which they had been working when the attack began.

Kurt edged toward the far side of the car.

"Do you want to come up here?" Mom asked.

"Come on, Kurt." Dad turned and held out his arms. Kurt pushed off with one tennis shoe from the seat behind him and slithered headfirst into the front. He quickly righted himself and took up a position on Mom's lap as far from the fighting as he could get.

"There's room for you, too, Keri." Dad tapped the padding over the gearbox.

"That's OK." Acting like she was afraid would be worse than saying the words. She dropped her arm over the back of the seat so it pressed against her father's shoulder. Her stomach felt like it was some place up around her heart, and maybe about ready to squeeze past and pop right out through her mouth. She hoped she wouldn't throw up.

"I have to go to the bathroom," said Kurt.

"Not now, Kurt." Dad pulled Keri firmly up against him and gripped her hand. "Let's pray," he said.

"I agree," said Mom. Keri recognized the deliberately controlled voice her mother used when Keri had lost her temper and Mom was trying not to lose hers.

"I'm already praying!" Kurt nodded emphatically.

Keri took her mother's hand as they always did for prayer. It felt cold and damp. Their arms were all tangled and crisscrossed in the car, not like the neat circle they made around the dining room table at home in Maputo. Everyone was touching everyone, and that was the way Keri wanted it right now.

"Help us, Lord God," her father prayed. "We don't know what's happening, but we know you do. We don't know what will happen, but we know we can trust you. Help us not to be frightened. Please protect us and bring us safely out of this, if it's your will. Protect the people of this village, too, and give this country peace. We'll give you all the glory. Amen."

Keri prayed with her eyes open. She thought God wouldn't mind if she watched what she was praying about. Her stomach seemed to settle back a few inches, and she was pretty sure it wouldn't pop out through her mouth after all. Her chest hurt where her heart thumped against her ribs.

Her father's eyes were also open. They both watched the

refugees from the village. Some of them had reached the *coluna*. They spread out along its length, putting the vehicles between themselves and the thick black smoke rising from the village beyond the hill. There were a couple hundred people, most of them women and children. Loud wails filled the air like a funeral. Kurt put his hands over his ears.

A woman with a baby on her back frantically questioned neighbors. A naked toddler clung to the hem of the cloth wrapped around her like a skirt. The *capulana* originally must have been printed with a bright red-orange pattern and black border, but it had faded to a pale gray and pinkish-pumpkin. Some neighbors merely shook their heads. Others pointed back toward the village. Whatever it was the woman searched for, she didn't find.

"Will Chibuto be like this?" asked Kurt. His voice sounded tight as if he might cry.

"No, sweetheart." Mom squeezed him on her lap. "Chibuto's a safe city. Pastor Makusa assured us that we won't go any place dangerous, and we'll always get back to Chibuto well before dark."

Keri had heard her father say how foolish it was to be outside the city at night. When they drove to the neighboring country of Swaziland to buy groceries every few months, they always traveled in the middle of the day. Even then, they would turn back if the soldiers at the checkpoints said it was dangerous.

Far ahead jeeps raced up the hill between the acacia trees. Foot soldiers swarmed toward the village. Spears of light brighter than day flashed from their guns in a rhythm that

18

seemed to have nothing to do with the delayed sounds that punctured the air. Straggling villagers fled both soldiers and bandits.

A soldier approached the Land Rover from the back reaches of the *coluna*. His AK47 was trained on the refugees streaming from the village. He hunched tensely over his gun, and Keri nervously remembered stories she had heard of inexperienced guards firing by mistake.

Kurt sat up straighter. "There're still some soldiers here." He pointed toward the young man's camouflaged uniform.

The driver of the yellow Peugeot opened his door and got out. He looked like a middle-aged Portuguese. Thinning gray hair covered his round head, and his belly hung over his belt. He called to the soldier, and the two talked excitedly.

Dad rolled down the window. Keri breathed deeply of the fresh air, but the men's voices were too far away to catch what was said.

"I'm going to see what's happening." Dad opened his door and jumped to the ground.

"Don't go!" begged Kurt, grasping his shirt.

"It's OK." Mom soothed him. "He won't go far."

Keri opened her door to follow.

"Keri! Stay here!" Mom's tone was not one Keri dared to disobey. She closed the door again and watched her father's back.

Dad had Kurt's stocky build. His khaki shorts and open-necked shirt made him look more like a big game hunter than the head of an African relief and development team.

The other man greeted Dad as though they had known each other for years. His gestures were wide and dramatic. He followed Dad back to the car and stood behind him, adding details in the whishing lilt of a Lisbon accent.

"The bandits attacked the village a few minutes before we got here," Dad explained to Mom. "Evidently, they expected the *coluna* to have already passed through." He glanced back over his shoulder. Four soldiers were pulling smoking thatch from the roof of a hut. "Our soldiers will drive them off." Dad looked apologetically at Mom. "He says this is the third time this month this has happened."

Behind him, the Portuguese man began an explicit story of the last attack he had seen, what the soldiers had done, and how many had been killed. Kurt seemed to shrink into Mom's side until there was nothing left of him but eyes. Dad put a hand on the man's back and guided him away from the car. Keri glanced at Mom and didn't dare to follow. She sat with her ear to the open window, but all she could hear was the wailing of the refugees and the sounds of gunfire from the hill.

All up and down the line, people got out of their vehicles to watch and wait and talk to the villagers. The woman in the orange *capulana* moved up the *coluna*. She questioned everyone she met.

"You know, this is exactly why we have to go to Chibuto," Mom explained in her teacher voice. "The bandits will steal what they can and destroy the rest. These poor people will be left with nothing."

"Do you suppose the clothes got there all right?" Keri

asked. She had helped her father and the workers from Africa Assistance fill the truck with bags of used clothing donated by people in North America. Two weeks helping distribute them to needy villagers had sounded like an adventure. Now it was scary to think of going where the bandits had been.

"There's a public phone in Chibuto. Pastor Makusa called last night to say the truck had arrived with no problems," Mom assured her.

"They don't have enough food in Gaza either, do they?" Kurt said.

"No, Kurt, they don't. Some of the trucks in this convoy are probably carrying corn and chickens. The only food in Mozambique right now is what the relief agencies like ours bring in."

Dad slid into his seat and smiled weakly at Mom. "Sorry about this," he said.

Keri wrapped her arms around her father's seat back. He smelled clean and minty like the antacids he always kept in his pocket. "Dad, you brought corn up one time, didn't you?"

"Yep." He shook his head at the memory. "Even an over-loaded truck wasn't enough. Each family only got food for a couple days. Kids littler than Kurt picked up grains of corn that had fallen in the dust. They didn't lose one kernel."

Thinking about hungry people made Keri flush with anger. War was so stupid. Each side claimed to be for the people, but it was the people who died and went naked and hungry. There was no reason for it that Keri could see— only selfishness and greed for power.

Usually the war seemed too far away to touch her. In the three years they had lived in Maputo, she had gotten used to the gunshots of nervous guards that they heard almost every night. It was scary when she lay in her bed and listened to the booming of heavy artillery from the other side of the bay. The first night she heard it, Dad sat on the edge of her bed and prayed with her. He told her the guns were far away, and it was only the water in between that made them sound so near. But he didn't go away until Keri had fallen asleep.

Keri seemed to be constantly holding her breath, waiting for something terrible that was just out of sight, not talking about it, pretending it wasn't there. She was proud that their family had come to Africa to help. She knew her parents wouldn't let anything really bad happen to her. But right now, if she let herself think about it, she would be more frightened than she'd ever been in her life.

The shooting grew more distant.

"I'm hungry," Kurt said.

"I suppose we could have lunch." Mom brought sandwiches out of the cooler. It felt odd to sit in the car eating peanut butter and jelly sandwiches and carrot sticks and listening to the war.

"Shall we read *The Silver Chair*?" Dad asked. He picked up at chapter 3 where they had left off last night, but no one could concentrate. Even Dad's voice sounded forced, and after a few pages he stopped.

The Portuguese man came over to talk and brought chocolate for Keri and Kurt. He told them all about his grown children in Portugal and the grandchildren he hadn't seen since they were babies.

The refugees sat on the side of the road or paced nervously up and down. The woman in the orange *capulana* stopped near the Andersons and sat on the ground with her legs straight out in front of her while she nursed her baby. Her face was tense. Her black hair was done in tight braids neatly tucked under. The toddler sat at her side in exactly the same position with his patient little face turned, like hers, to the hill.

Suddenly the woman leapt to her feet, shouting and waving frantically. There was a responding shout, and a boy about Kurt's age appeared, running amidst the scanty shrubbery at the foot of the hill. He bounded toward her over rocks and around bushes. He wore only a pair of ragged shorts, and his dark legs and bare, callused feet were thickly covered with yellow dust. His mother shouted at him and boxed his ears when he came close, as if her worry had been replaced by anger that he should have scared her so.

Keri found herself grinning. Out of the corner of her eye she saw Kurt relax and readjust his position on Mom's lap. Mom squeezed him and gave him a kiss on the cheek. "I love you," she said. "Both of you."

At last the sounds of gunfire ceased. The jeeps made their way back down the hill, and foot soldiers returned to the waiting trucks. Keri took a deep breath and settled back on the seat. Everything was going to be OK. The bandits hadn't come near them. Their family was safe.

"Thank you, Lord," Dad prayed as he started the motor.

The *coluna* slowly moved forward as clusters of villagers straggled across the hillside to discover what was left of their homes. Keri felt a pang of guilt. Not everything was OK. Not for everyone. Her eyes darted here and there trying to find the woman in the orange *capulana* and her children among the figures climbing the hill. To leave not knowing what became of them felt like not reading the last chapter of a book, or turning off a television program five minutes before the end.

They're real people, Keri thought. *Not book people or TV people.*

"I hope their house wasn't burned," Kurt said. Keri didn't have to ask whom he meant.

CHAPTER 2

Home school was done for the morning. Keri stood at the brink of the hill at the edge of Chibuto and drank in the vision of Africa spread before her. The river traced a winding blue ribbon through the wide valley below. On either bank, tiny green gardens shaped themselves to the curve of the land. Rich black dirt showed between neat rows of corn and rice.

This was not the forsaken no-man's-land the *coluna* had traveled through. Nor was it anything like the broken glass and crumbling cement of Maputo. The war rarely allowed the Andersons to escape the capitol city, and Keri's soul was thirsty enough to soak up the whole Limpopo River. She drew deep breaths of sunshine and cloudless sky.

"I've never done this before, you know, Rute," Keri warned the African girl ahead of her. Pastor Makusa's granddaughter barely reached Keri's shoulder even though she was a year older. Her voice was rich and deep, and her wiry black hair was cut close like a boy's. The only way Keri could tell she was a girl was the faded cotton dress she wore.

Rute shrugged. Her bare feet stirred up little dust clouds in the path to the spring. Keri followed, swinging a battered kettle that looked embarrassingly small next to the five-gallon tin balanced on Rute's hip.

The girls stepped into the tall yellow grass at the side of the path to let a woman pass. The grass tickled Keri's legs under her denim skirt. She wished the country people didn't believe it was indecent for girls to wear jeans or shorts.

The woman coming up the path balanced on her head a tin the size of Rute's, brimming with water. Her arms swung loosely at her sides. Behind her was a little girl of six or seven. The child imitated her mother's graceful movements while one hand secured a restaurant-size margarine tin on her head.

A toddler trailed them on chubby legs. She firmly held a small soup can of water on her head with both little hands. She jerked at every step. Half the water had already spilled over her round cheeks and shapeless mud-colored dress.

Keri giggled. "That's what I'll do," she said. "I'm no better than a two year old!" She balanced the kettle on her head and tried to walk, but the movement of her steps sent it rolling into a clump of weeds.

Rute said nothing, but her eyes danced with amusement.

Keri retrieved the kettle. She stood up straight and, with mock seriousness, repositioned it on her head. This time she held it with one hand like the first little girl imitating her mother. Even empty, the bottom felt hard and uncomfortable against her skull.

"You don't have to carry it on your head," Rute assured

her, her voice full of laughter. She turned and started down the path.

Scores of bright cloths and small pieces of drying clothing littered the hillside bushes. Women and children bathed and did laundry in the rocky pools beneath the spring. They didn't seem the least bit shy about bathing naked in front of other people.

An iron pipe stuck out of a rocky outcropping in the hill and spilled its flow into a shallow pool. A long line of women talked and gossiped while they waited their turn. Rute started to go to the end of the line. The women laughed and chattered in Shangana, the local language. They motioned the girls to the front. One reached out and stroked Keri's straight yellow hair.

Keri felt her cheeks turn red. "I don't want to take cuts!" she said.

"We could wait for hours if we don't," Rute reminded her in her practical way. "Come on."

Rute set her five-gallon container under the pipe. Water crashed against the bottom. She pulled handfuls of long grass and twisted it into a ring as she chatted with the women.

Women and children from the washing pools came to watch. A crowd of little boys stared as though Keri were an exotic animal in the zoo.

"*Olá*," said Keri to a naked baby, bouncing on his sister's hip. The child set up a wail, and his sister backed away. The little boys jabbered and pointed.

"I'm sorry!" Keri didn't know which was worse—to be stared at or run from.

"How did you learn Portuguese?" she asked Rute.

"I go to school," Rute explained.

Keri looked around. "Don't the other children go to school?"

Rute made a disparaging gesture. "They don't like school. They only speak Shangana at home, so they can't understand the teacher and they fail. My grandfather speaks Portuguese to me sometimes, so I understand."

"What about your parents?"

Rute shrugged. "They're dead."

"Oh."

When Rute's container was nearly full, she slid it aside and wedged Keri's kettle under the flow. She pulled handfuls of grass and spread them on the surface of the water.

"Why are you doing that?" Keri asked in surprise.

"It helps to hold the water steady," Rute explained. She pulled a scarf from her pocket and twisted it into a roll similar to the one she had made of grass. She placed the rolled-up scarf on Keri's head and helped her to lift the full kettle. It weighed a lot more than it had empty, but the scarf kept it from pressing down on her skull. The watching women roared with friendly laughter and encouragement.

Keri giggled, and water spilled down the back of her neck. "Yipes! That's cold." She jerked and spilled half the kettle on her blouse and skirt. The women laughed harder than ever. Keri wished they weren't all looking at her.

A woman in a bright green headscarf with one of her front teeth missing took the kettle in her strong hands. She refilled it from the spring and re-placed it on Keri's head.

Keri tried to motion that she would carry it in her hands, but the women wouldn't hear of it.

Rute grinned broadly as she placed the grass ring she had made on her own head. One of the women helped the African girl hoist the heavy kerosene tin and rest it on the soft grass padding. Rute turned in a smooth graceful movement and started up the trail.

It's part of the adventure, Keri told herself, repeating a phrase her mother often used. Water sloshed down her back with each awkward step. A handful of children crowded around, laughing and shouting. They turned back to tell tales when halfway up the trail, Keri shifted the kettle to her hand. It banged painfully against her leg. Even that was less uncomfortable than the constant dousing.

From the sandy lane, the girls slipped through the bamboo fence to the yard of Pastor Makusa's house. It was one of the few houses in the neighborhood built of cement block. The family was proud of the glass in the living room window. The naked bulb that hung from the ceiling had given a weak orange glow for a few hours last evening.

Keri followed Rute through the activity of the yard and left the water in the outdoor kitchen. Rute stayed to wash the dishes, bending over a pottery bowl wedged in the sand. She rubbed a fibrous plant in a dish of soft gray soap to use as a sponge. One of the aunts shooed Keri away, and returned to stirring thick porridge in an iron pot over the fire. Evidently she didn't think it was dignified for a visitor to help.

"I'm playing *coluna*." Kurt scooted in the sand marking a two-tracked trail with his fingers. "You can play, too."

Keri wasn't sure she wanted to play *coluna*. After their adventures on the road, it didn't sound like a nice game.

"Did you finish your social studies?" she asked suspiciously. Mom had made him stay after to finish answering the questions at the end of the chapter.

"Yeah," he said. "C'mon, Keri. Help me find things to be the cars and trucks."

In all their moves to different parts of Africa, Kurt had been her constant companion. Even if he was six years younger, sometimes there simply wasn't anyone else. Keri sighed and looked around.

The yard was as sandy as a beach. It had been raked clean, and it wasn't easy to find bits of rubbish or pieces of wood. She found a curved length of bark in the woodpile and pulled some wide leaves from the mango tree. Mom sat with Pastor Makusa's wife on a reed mat under the tree, shelling dry corn. Her slender figure looked girlish next to *Mamani* Jordina's broad bulk.

"Hi, Keri." Mom's face lit in a smile. "Did you do any better carrying water than I'm doing shelling corn?" She frowned at her thumb and sucked the side of it.

"I got pretty wet," Keri admitted.

"We're not very good Africans, are we? I think I'm getting a blister." Mom's pile of corn was much smaller than *Mamani* Jordina's. "Oh, well. It's part of the adventure."

"*Bom dia, Mamani,*" Keri greeted the pastor's wife. *Mamani* Jordina didn't speak Portuguese, but she understood a little. She showed her white teeth in a broad grin under her brightly patterned headscarf, and said "*Bom dia*" in the awkward voice of someone playing with a foreign language.

Keri pointed to an empty corncob and asked for it with her eyes. *Mamani* Jordina looked surprised. Keri pointed to Kurt and tried to explain in words she knew would not be understood.

"What are you playing?" Mom asked.

"Kurt wants to build a *coluna*."

"Oh." Mom looked across the yard at Kurt as though she didn't like the sound of that any more than Keri did.

Mamani Jordina handed Keri the cob with both hands. Keri clapped her hands together to show her thanks and moved on. The cob could be a tank truck.

"*Olá, Keri!*" André, the young church secretary, lifted a large plastic bag of used clothing onto the head of a woman. She joined the line of women carrying similar bundles from the thatched storage shed to the Land Rover. André grinned and his eyes twinkled like he would rather play with the children, but he had no time to talk. Her father and Pastor Makusa stood nearby.

"All these clothes will be such a relief to the villagers," Pastor Makusa said. His black face glowed. "They have been robbed and burned out so many times. They have nothing left, and we have nothing left to give them."

"We saw that firsthand," Dad agreed. He smiled at Keri, and she leaned against him. He reached around her and gave her shoulders a soft squeeze while he talked. She breathed his minty smell.

"I am so sorry," Pastor Makusa apologized.

He was a grandfatherly man whose suit coat didn't quite meet over his rounded middle. His narrow maroon tie might have been stylish in America some time before Keri was born. In the three days the Andersons had been in Chibuto, she had never seen him dress any other way. He had apologized over and over for the problems on the road. The elders had canceled yesterday's village distribution because it was too near rebel territory. Tomorrow would be their first trip out.

A red plastic basin and a wooden scrub brush sat on a bench bleached white and smooth from years of laundry soap. Keri slid out from under her father's arm.

"May we borrow that brush?" she asked politely in Portuguese. "We'll put it back when we're done."

"*Claro!*" The pastor picked up the brush and pressed it into her hands with both of his.

"'*Brigada*," she replied. She bobbed a curtsey as she had seen Rute do.

The older man turned back to her father. "There were only a few shoes or sport coats on the truck," he explained as she walked away. "The elders have spent long hours deciding which of the chiefs have the greatest need."

Kurt's eyes lit up at the sight of the scrub brush. "That can be a truck load of soldiers!" he said. "They're all standing packed in the back like the ones on our *coluna*."

Keri still didn't like this game. It was too much like talking about what had happened. She didn't want to talk about it. She didn't want to remember how her stomach felt when the guns were shooting, and there was nothing they could do but sit there and listen. She pressed one arm over her stomach and clipped the ends off three fingernails with her teeth while Kurt arranged the things she had found in a line along the road he had made.

"There's the village," Kurt said. He pointed to where he had heaped sand in small piles a little ahead of the *coluna*. "The bandits attacked, and we're the soldiers!" The little boy gripped an imaginary machine gun and raked the village with its fire. "Uh-uh-uh-uh-uh-uh!" His bare feet kicked up sand as he pranced around it.

Keri's stomach turned a somersault. "Stop!" She gripped her brother's arm. Flying sand stung her legs, and she raised her arm to protect her eyes.

"Let go!" Kurt shook her off. "No armed bandits are going to get this *coluna*!" He filled the air with his imitation machine gun sounds. "Uh-uh-uh-uh-uh-uh!"

CHAPTER 3

Early the next morning they piled into the Land Rover.

"Here, Keri." Mom tossed Keri the backpack of snacks and emergency supplies. She lifted the front of her loose denim skirt and swung herself nimbly into the back of the cab with the children.

Pastor Makusa sat in the front with Dad. André rode in the back with bags of clothes.

"No schoolwork today!" Kurt announced gleefully.

"This is a field trip," Mom explained. Keri had an uncomfortable suspicion she would be asked to write a composition on it tomorrow. Even that couldn't diminish her sense of adventure.

They stopped twice for government checkpoints. After politely answering the soldier's brief questions, Pastor Makusa gave him a little gift of high protein biscuits from UNESCO and a piece of soap. "They get dropped off out here for days without supplies," he explained. A few hundred meters after the second checkpoint, they turned off the gravel road onto a dirt track.

"This road was swept for mines just last week," Pastor

Makusa said. "We had to get official permission to travel here." Keri thought he was saying that to reassure them, but it made her nervous. She worked at the nail on her right thumb until she tore it off with her teeth.

The bush was sparse on either side. Here and there were flat-topped acacia trees looking like giant tables draped with lacy green tablecloths. The grass beneath them was so sparse that Keri could see each individual blade. They made a pale green fuzz against the golden brown of the earth and made her think of the baby hairs on Grandpa's bare scalp.

"Look!" Kurt shouted. "A monkey!" Suddenly the bush was alive with gray monkeys with tiny black and white faces. They scurried away from the noisy Land Rover.

Keri bounced excitedly. "Will we see more wild animals?"

"Probably not many," her mother explained. "The buck and warthogs have all been eaten, no doubt."

Disappointed, Keri searched the bush just in case. She was rewarded by being the first to spot a thorn tree with dozens of weaver nests hanging like fruit from its branches.

"How do they keep from getting scratched?" Kurt asked as the brilliant yellow birds darted in and out. He fingered the scar on his arm from his own encounter with the two-inch thorns.

"I have no idea." Mom shook her head in awe.

When they arrived in the village they were met by a man no taller than Keri who never seemed to stop moving.

"This is Pastor Ndima," Pastor Makusa introduced him. Ndima led them with a bouncy step to a shadowy building with a dirt floor. A small tree supported the roof. Before she knew it, Keri was standing by the trunk in front of a line of women, all fidgeting with excitement. Her job was to decide if the next woman needed a large blouse or a small blouse and give her one from the right pile.

She held a green one to the shoulders of a grandmotherly woman. It didn't fit at all. The blue checked one that was next in the pile appeared to fit better. The woman's pleased smile showed the gaps of two missing teeth. Keri felt a warm glow of pleasure.

After she got a blouse, each woman turned to Mom who often had to hold up several dresses before finding one that might fit. No one worried about the length since the woman would tie a *capulana* over it most of the time. Mozambican women always wore the long printed cloth even if they turned it inside out for an apron.

Dad and Kurt handed out shirts to the men. Pastor Ndima supervised the distribution of trousers. He was wearing the blue plaid sport coat Pastor Makusa had brought him. André, the secretary, ran errands and kept them supplied with bags from the car. Pastor Makusa paid visits and delivered shoes to the headmen.

The next woman in line grinned expectantly at Keri. Her huge breasts looked like watermelons under her blouse. Keri gulped and reached for the pile of large sizes. The first blouse was far too small. The woman laughed. Keri held up the next one. The grin began to fade.

"Just a minute! I'll find something," Keri assured her even though she knew the woman couldn't understand her. She didn't want anyone to go away disappointed. A bit of light blue crochet work showed near the bottom of the pile. Crochet would stretch.

"There! That should fit." She held it up. The smile was back as the woman turned to Mom.

Kurt's face bent earnestly over the few shirts that remained while he searched for one that might fit the skinny teenager in front of him.

"Why aren't there any clothes for kids?" he asked in English.

"Kids wear out their clothes," Keri said. "Or hand them down to their cousins or something. Only grown-ups buy new clothes when their old ones are still perfectly good."

"But if they didn't," Kurt reminded her, "we wouldn't have anything to give away." He gave the boy the smallest shirt he could find. It was wool flannel and looked awfully hot for Africa. "I'm hungry," he went on.

"There's dried fruit and trail mix in Mom's backpack," Keri reminded him. She was hungry, too. It was three o'clock in the afternoon, and the line had not stopped for lunch.

"Naw, I'll wait," Kurt said.

The last woman filed past, and Keri gathered up the half dozen remaining blouses and returned them to the bag. The last of the villagers left the shelter.

"Come, and we will take a cup of water together in my house," Pastor Ndima invited.

Kurt's eyes grew wide. "Only a cup of water?" he whispered to Keri. "I'm hungrier than that!"

"Hush! He's just being humble," Keri said. "It'll probably be stewed chicken just like in Chibuto." Keri used to like chicken, but after eating it the same way twice every day, she was getting tired of it.

The children filed behind their parents into Pastor Ndima's tiny house. The center room was nearly filled with a large Portuguese style dining table and chairs. A loosely woven mat nailed over the unglazed window for privacy made it dim and cool. Its grassy scent mingled with the smell of stewed chicken. A calendar from several years ago decorated one wall.

There was only a little tomato in the chicken, and no other seasoning. Keri added salt from an enamel plate full of large crystals. They were bigger than the ones Grandma used for pickles back in Minnesota, and they didn't mix in too well.

The village elders joined them, heaping their plates and making appreciative sounds over the meat. They teased Dad when he brought a little hand filter out of the backpack and pumped river water through it, but Keri noticed that they all drank the sparkling clear water instead of the water with brown floating specks from the pitcher. When the clean water ran out, they took turns joking and pumping more.

There were no women at the table except Mom and no other children in sight. *They probably got stiff porridge with those nice pumpkin greens I saw the women cooking this afternoon*, Keri thought. She toyed with her piece of stringy chicken. To Africans, meat was a special treat to be served to company. She would have much preferred porridge with pumpkin greens in peanut sauce. It wasn't so chewy or slimy in your mouth.

"The situation in the outlying parts of the district is much better than it was a few months ago," Pastor Makusa said to Dad.

Keri recognized the word "situation." What he really meant was "war," but the adults never used that word. It was as if they knew that if you didn't talk about it, it wouldn't be so scary.

"This very village was attacked in June."

Their host nodded. "I was sitting here preparing my sermon when I heard the shots," Pastor Ndima explained. "I left my books spread on the table and fled. No one else was home. I prayed, 'God protect my children and my books.' You know how hard it is for us to get books."

Dad nodded.

Keri could see a Portuguese Bible and a songbook in the local African dialect on the shelf in the corner. There were less than half a dozen other volumes in the pastor's library. She shivered, wondering what it would be like to run for your life and not know what was happening to your family. What would she ask God to protect if she had to run? Her family first. That was for sure. Somehow her sticker collection or the stuffed lamb she had had since she was a baby didn't seem as important anymore.

The African pastor went on. "I caught up with my wife and three of my children on the road. When I got to Chibuto, I found the others had come with relatives. All were safe." The small man shook his head and clicked his tongue as though he could still hardly believe his good fortune.

"When we were able to come home, all our clothes and food supplies had been stolen, but my books were still on the table where I had left them." He grinned and patted the spot where they had lain. "My Bible had been moved as though someone had picked it up to look at and then put it back. But it was here."

There were murmurs of approval around the table.

"Have church people been killed in the attacks?" Dad asked.

The other men grew quiet. Pastor Makusa's face looked old in the lantern light. He spoke slowly, nodding his head for emphasis and pausing between each sentence. "Many have died. Some have starved. Some have been caught by the bandits and killed. Some have been carried off to be wives for the rebel soldiers or porters to carry the stolen goods. Sometimes people are killed in their beds and their goods burned for no apparent reason. It happens to good people as well as to bad." He paused.

The scrape of Kurt's fork on his plate sounded loud in the silence. Keri crossed her feet under the table to keep from kicking him to be quiet.

"I lost some of my own family that way," the pastor went on.

Dad murmured sympathetically, and Keri felt like a lump of unchewed chicken was stuck in her throat.

"I come originally from a village to the west of here," Pastor Makusa explained. "It is a beautiful land where the Limpopo makes a large sweep around a flat-topped hill. There is plenty of water for crops and good grazing on the steep slopes.

40

"My two sons lived on farms next to mine. When I came to Chibuto to pastor the church, they took care of my land. I brought Rute, my oldest granddaughter, to help my wife and go to school."

Keri remembered what Rute had said about her parents being dead. Her hands turned cold. She wiped the sweat on her skirt.

"Not long after that," Pastor Makusa continued, "one son died of malaria. Rute's father built a new hut in his homestead and brought his brother's widow and her children to live there. Just after the harvest the bandits came. They stole all the grain and set the houses on fire while everyone slept. All are dead but Rute—my children and six grandchildren, including a new baby we had never seen."

Keri stared at the chicken broth puddled on her plate. Closing her eyes couldn't shut out the memories of flames lapping thatch or sobbing refugees.

"Only one grandchild's body was not found. We do not know what happened to him. He was the oldest boy, Dzumisana. He was seven years old—just your age." The old man looked at Kurt. "He used to tend the goats on the side of the hill and bring them to a little corral at night. Surely he died too, but the bodies were so badly burned we couldn't tell." He shook his head sorrowfully.

"How sad," Mom said softly. "Dzumisana means 'Let us give praise,' doesn't it? What a beautiful name! How long ago was this? Perhaps he fled and will make his way to you in Chibuto like Pastor Ndima's children."

The old man shook his head. "It has been five years now

since they died. I clung to hope for a while, but it has been too long."

Five years, thought Keri. Dzumisana would have grown and changed. Would Pastor Makusa even know his grandson if he met him?

The pastor smiled a wise smile. "God doesn't always answer 'yes' to our prayers. We don't know why. He let Job suffer in the Bible, and Job never knew why."

His face was deeply lined. "This world is full of sin and suffering. Christ died for our sin, and in His death He shared our suffering." He paused and murmured almost to himself, "Dzumisana! Let us give praise!"

CHAPTER 4

Keri was bored. She was tired of the constant vibration of the Land Rover. They were on their way to the second village visit of the day, and the car raced much too quickly over the ruts and bumps of the road. They were late.

They had eaten a hurried meal in the first village. The Africans wouldn't consider it a real visit unless they ate.

"I wish they would give us beans or pumpkin greens instead of slimy chicken all the time," Kurt had complained. Keri agreed.

An hour later Keri shifted uncomfortably on the sweaty seat. She had stopped being nervous when Pastor Makusa talked about mines in the road or "the situation." Nothing ever happened—just driving and handing out clothes and eating stewed chicken.

Kurt pulled a wadded piece of cloth from his pocket and unwrapped it. He took out a tiny carved ox and began to move it slowly across the top of the front seat as though it were grazing.

"Where'd you get that?" Keri asked.

"*Vovô Pastor* made him for me," Kurt said, pointing at the broad back of Pastor Makusa in front of him.

"Grandpa Pastor?" Keri asked.

"That's what he said I could call him," Kurt said. "He's my friend."

Although they were speaking English, the pastor turned at the sound of his name in Portuguese and smiled when he saw the ox.

"Let *me* see." Keri held out her hand.

Kurt handed over the ox. The fat little animal had been carefully fashioned from a knobby branch of shrub. Four sturdy legs stuck out. Two dry sprouts looked exactly like horns. The knob formed the hump typical on the backs of African cattle. Tiny eyes and nostrils burned into the wood brought the animal to life.

Keri looked up as they rounded a curve. A deep hole loomed in the road. The bush closed in thickly on either side. There was no place to swerve. Keri ducked instinctively. The Land Rover plunged into the hole and bounded wildly out the other side.

"Whee!" cried Kurt as he rose in the air.

For one moment gravity seemed suspended. Even ducking her head Keri felt the back of it brush against the thin steel roof. It was fun. Pastor Makusa smiled but maintained his quiet dignity even as he reached out a hand to steady himself on the dashboard.

Loud scraping noises came from the bottom of the car. The motor roared, and Kurt clapped his hands over his ears. The vehicle banged and shook. Abruptly, the noise stopped.

Keri looked back through the window to be sure André was all right. The young man knocked on the glass and pointed back the way they had come.

There in the middle of the road lay not only the muffler but also the entire exhaust system.

"Uh, oh," Dad moaned as he reversed the Land Rover. He pulled as far off the road as he could, but the way was still blocked.

Mom chuckled. "We haven't seen another vehicle for hours! If someone comes along now, we *want* him to stop!"

No one came.

Dad and André pulled out some bags of clothing so that they could get to the toolbox under the seat in the back of the Land Rover. André crawled under the car.

"It isn't far to the village," Pastor Makusa suggested. "If we could get there then André could work on the car while we distribute the clothing."

André stuck his grease-streaked face out from under the vehicle and waited respectfully for his elders to make a decision.

"What do you think, André? Can you fix it?" Dad asked. He popped something in his mouth. When he bit down, Keri smelled the mint of his antacids.

"It will take some time," the young man replied.

"Can we drive it?"

André looked thoughtful. "As long as it doesn't overheat."

"Then let's go for the village."

They crept along at a maddeningly slow pace. "Not far" took a lot longer than Keri had expected. The African meaning for the expression wasn't very precise. She saw Pastor Makusa glancing nervously at the position of the sun. They would be hard-pressed to get back to Chibuto before dark.

"Do you think we should be going on?" Dad asked Pastor Makusa. In deference to Dad's position, the African would never volunteer his opinion.

The older man shook his head slowly. "I don't think we have a choice. The Land Rover won't make it back to Chibuto, and there is no place to sleep in between."

Keri wondered if they would have to camp in the bush that night. A shiver of fear went down her back. *The Africans sleep in the bush all the time,* she reminded herself. *It's safer than the houses during the war.* She gripped a fingernail in her teeth and tore at it.

After what seemed like forever, Keri spotted a tall gangly boy in the road ahead, trailed by a group of smaller boys. When he saw them, the boy turned and ran around a bend in the road, waving his long thin arms, scattering the other children.

"Listen," instructed Pastor Makusa.

Over the unmuffled engine noises they could hear African singing, wild and rhythmic. They rounded the corner and were stopped by a colorful mass of dancing people. All were clapping or waving branches of leaves. The women made a shrill sound through quivering lips. It pierced Keri with joyful excitement.

"We may be tired, but they're just getting started," Dad said with a laugh as the car crept into the crowd.

"Come up here where you can see better," Pastor Makusa

suggested to Kurt. The boy slid over the seat and settled in the big man's lap as naturally as if he had belonged there all his life.

They rolled down the windows. Eager children reached in to shake hands.

Keri laughed and shook as many of the hands thrust at her as she could manage. Kurt shrank back against *Vovô Pastor* until the old man had shaken a few hands, and Kurt began to imitate him.

Wrinkled old ladies waggled their hips and bounced up and down to the rhythms of the vibrant song. Men flung their arms over their heads and whirled in time. Drums beat and a whistle pulsed. The gangly boy who had been watching out for them kicked his feet as high as his head to the intense beat. He danced directly in front of the Land Rover, clearing a space for them to move as he led them down the road toward the village. Keri sat forward, and her feet beat the infectious rhythm on the floor of the car.

As they approached the village itself, they were met by yet another group of people that thronged out and merged into their enthusiastic escort like the flow of two rivers joining. They were surrounded by a sea of smiling brown faces and moving bodies.

"Stop the car," suggested Pastor Makusa, "and let us join them."

The moment the doors were open Keri felt a half dozen friendly hands help her from the seat. The acrid smell of warm bodies flowed over her. It wasn't an unpleasant smell—just an authentic people smell. Laughing voices whose words were incomprehensible to her urged her to the front. In a moment she found herself walking beside her mother in a circle of calm with Kurt clinging excitedly to the other side. The rhythm still pulsed in her heart, but she held her body firmly controlled. She was too embarrassed to let the music spill out when she was the center of attention.

Mom took her hand and began to move her feet in a simple African dance step. Keri jerked her foot down on Mom's at the exact same instant as Kurt did on the other side. Mom tripped and caught herself with a laugh.

"Don't you want to join in?" she asked.

"No," they replied firmly in unison.

"Where's your sense of adventure?" Mom shook her head and walked between them, but there was a bounce in her step.

Keri glanced back over her shoulder to look at her father who guided the Land Rover inch by inch behind them. In front of them, the high-kicking boy led the way. Beside him Pastor Makusa, despite his age, seemed to have lost all his accustomed dignity. His wide grin split his glowing face wide open, and he proudly displayed the dancing skills of his youth. Although he lacked the energy of the boy beside him, he showed no less enthusiasm. The villagers sang louder and more vigorously.

At last Dad drew the car to a stop beside a temporary tin roofed shelter in the heart of the village, and the crowd quieted to listen to instructions on how the distribution would be conducted.

Despite the chaotic confusion of the welcome, the women were soon filing past Keri in an orderly line. Their clothes were threadbare, and they were delighted with the blouses she gave them.

Only one woman seemed less than pleased. A silky black blouse was the next on the pile when her turn came. She shifted the fussy toddler on her hip, and gave her head an almost invisible shake. Her eyes fixed intently at the next one down. It was pale pink scattered with tiny roses. Black is for mourning, Keri realized. It would be bad luck to give someone a black blouse if she didn't need it. She set it aside for someone who did.

The smell of wood smoke and cooking beans filled the late afternoon air.

"I hope the food is ready," Dad said when the last villager had gone through the line. Pastor Makusa was presenting a green sport coat two sizes too big to the local chief. "We need to be on our way as soon as possible."

"Is the car fixed?" Keri asked. There was no sign of André near the Land Rover.

Pastor Makusa turned to Dad, all his previous dignity restored.

"We will sleep here tonight," he announced. "André was unable to fix the car. The parts are rusted through. The chief loaned him a bicycle and sent him to the next village. There's a mechanic there, and even if they don't have parts, there will be a car that can go back to Chibuto for them. I'm afraid he won't be back before tomorrow at the earliest."

Dad took a deep breath. His hand reached in the pocket

where he kept the antacids. "All right," he said slowly. Keri knew he always tried to follow the advice of the African leaders. She couldn't see that they had much choice this time.

"The meal is ready, and Chief Mbuluzi's wives are preparing a place for us to sleep."

"At least we won't have to worry about clean clothes for tomorrow." Mom lifted the plastic bag in her hand with a half dozen leftover garments.

But it was the clothes that brought on the attack.

CHAPTER 5

The late afternoon light was turning to gold as they entered the large *rondavel* to share the chief's hospitality. Keri giggled when she noticed the bright plastic toothbrushes stuck conveniently in the thatch over the door. A slender girl, so dark she almost disappeared in the shadows, held out a basin and pitcher for them to wash their hands.

"*Obrigada*," said Mom. "I'm almost glad we aren't trying to drive home," she murmured to Dad. "We'd be alone on the road. At least here we'll be with friends."

"It wasn't our choice," Dad replied. "God's in control even when we feel so out of control. Don't let me forget that." He washed his hands and dried them on the towel that hung on the girl's arm.

Keri followed. She smiled, and the girl smiled shyly back. Keri had never thought about anything being out of control for grown-ups. Her father was an important man. He spoke at conferences and had university degrees. It seemed like he always knew the right thing to do. Her stomach had a funny up-in-the-air feeling. Maybe it was just hunger.

The traditional round house was divided into two rooms. A large dining table and chairs filled the front room. A kerosene lantern on the table cast weird shadows on the clay walls.

Pastor Makusa, as guest of honor, had entered first and sat at the far end of the table. He had Kurt by his side. Dad was seated on the other side of Pastor Makusa, and Mom was directed to the seat beside him. Keri hoped she would be allowed to follow. The order of seating in Africa was very important, and she had been taught not to presume. Chief Mbuluzi smiled at Keri and nodded for her to follow her mother. Church elders and village dignitaries took up the other places. There were no other women or children.

A faded cotton cloth covered the table. Two plates were turned upside down on it in front of each person. That meant there would be more than one course—something besides stewed chicken!

Pastor Makusa turned over his plates. Everyone else did the same. The young woman entered with a large enamel soup tureen painted with a bright orange poppy. She must be one of Chief Mbuluzi's daughters. She set the tureen on the table and then bowed her head for the grace.

The words were mumbled so low that Keri couldn't have heard them even if she understood the language. It didn't matter. She knew the girl was asking that there be enough to feed all those who would eat and that no one would get sick from it.

"Amen," murmured the girl.

"Amen," answered all those at the table.

The tureen was passed to Pastor Makusa. When he removed the lid, the rich aroma of bean soup filled the room.

Keri smiled eagerly. Her favorite. The soup was made by simmering sugar beans on a wood fire, pounding them with stampers in a hollowed out log and then straining the stock back into the pot. Keri wondered where the few bits of macaroni that floated in the thick, reddish brown broth had come from this far from the city. It would have been nicer with a little tomato, onion, and greens like they served it in Maputo, but the broth had the strong scent of wood smoke that she and Kurt loved.

The adults talked about the "situation," the drought, and the refugees. The children scraped their plates and stared hard at the tureen. Mom noticed and whispered to Dad.

"Is there more soup in the tureen?" Dad asked the other end of the table.

"A little," came the reply, and it was passed. Keri knew very well that the dignitaries would rather fill up on the chicken and porridge that was coming. They probably hadn't eaten meat since the last visitors, whenever that was.

"You may divide it," Dad said. Kurt shoved his plate eagerly across, and Keri measured what was left into two equal portions.

The soup plates were removed, and platters of white, grainy, stiff porridge were brought to the table along with a bowl of the inevitable stewed chicken. Pastor Makusa heaped Kurt's plate with porridge.

"Ah, a special piece for my grandson," he said putting a chicken leg on Kurt's plate. The last scaly joint and the foot were still attached. Kurt stared at the stiffly spread toes with their curled claws.

Keri stifled a giggle.

Pastor Makusa served himself the other foot and passed the bowl to Dad. The elderly African broke the foot off the drumstick and put one end in his mouth. He crunched the bones and sucked through his teeth with a delighted expression on his face. At last he spit the mass of chewed bones into his hand and laid it neatly at the edge of his porridge.

"Mmm," he said. He started to dip his fingers into the porridge, but remembered just in time and picked up his fork.

Keri saw Kurt look helplessly at Dad who gave him a you-will-eat-that look. Kurt looked back at his plate.

"You may suck on it," Mom said quietly in English. "You don't have to chew the bones."

Bet he's glad he had seconds on soup, Keri thought.

"I have to go to the bathroom," Kurt said a little later in English. Keri could see the leftover foot bones sticking out of the excess porridge on his plate.

"Do you know where it is?" Mom asked.

"I do," Keri offered. Although the door stood open, there were no windows, and the lantern made the air hot and stuffy.

"Take the flashlight," Dad suggested. He dug in the backpack under his seat and pulled it out.

The young woman came in with a tray of cups and a battered aluminum kettle of hot water that smelled more of lemon than of tea. Keri and Kurt slipped past her into the night.

The sun had gone down while they were inside. The trees and peaked huts of the village showed black against deepening purple sky as Keri led the way to the outhouse. The flashlight cast eerie shadows along the path between the huts. The brightness of its yellow beam made the darkness beyond its reach deeper and more profound. Kurt took her hand.

"There it is." She pointed to an enclosure that gleamed white out of the darkness. The grassy scent of newly cut cane tickled her nose. The latrine pit had been freshly dug for the use of the visitors. Keri had seen women with branches shooing children away from it during the afternoon. It didn't smell anything like an outhouse.

Kurt held back. "You come, too," he said.

"I'll wait here. You take the light," she offered.

That seemed to satisfy him.

Keri waited outside in the deepening darkness. A group of women sat around a dying fire a short distance away. *They're probably the ones that cooked for us.* She could see the glow of other fires and hear the murmur of quiet voices through the night. The only other sound was the long, steady stream of Kurt doing his business behind the screen.

The sky was filled with millions of tiny stars. Keri thought if she reached out far enough she would prick her fingers on their sharp points. A crowded bridge of white arched from one horizon to the other—the Milky Way. The stars were so much brighter away from town. There was a feeling of peace and contentment about the village at the end of an eventful day.

By the time Kurt came out of the enclosure, her eyes had grown accustomed to the night.

"Leave the light off," she instructed.

"It's dark," Kurt complained.

"Turn it off and look at the stars."

Kurt turned it off. He tilted his fair head back to look where Keri pointed. Keri heard his breath slowly being let out beside her. She reached for his hand, and the two of them stood side by side admiring the glittering heavens.

They were still standing that way when they heard the first shots.

"What was that?" Kurt asked, gripping his sister's arm.

"Probably just nervous guards shooting at stray dogs," she said. They heard the sound nearly every night at home in Maputo. Then she remembered she hadn't seen any dogs all day.

The women by the fire leaped to their feet. One of them grabbed up a bundle from the ground and all of them ran toward the sparse woods behind them.

Screams came from the village but no more shots.

"Mama!" yelled Kurt and broke away from Keri's grasp.

"Kurt!" She was sure they should be running toward the bush with the women. They would find their parents later in Chibuto like Pastor Ndima's children. But Kurt was running toward the cluster of houses.

Dimly out of the darkness, Keri saw figures moving in from the surrounding forest.

Armed bandits! They hadn't seen her yet. She raced after Kurt into the labyrinth of narrow lanes between the huts.

In the starlight, everything took on the vague confusion of a dream. She was temporarily blinded by looking toward an abandoned cooking fire and stumbled. Her groping hand touched something hard and long in the sand. The flashlight! Kurt had come this way. She picked herself up. The flashlight was in her hand, but she didn't turn it on. She didn't want to draw attention to herself or destroy what little night vision she had.

In front of her were running figures. The sound of gunfire and flashes of orange piercing the night like knives told her that they were not all villagers. She hung back. Behind her were the sounds of wailing and of struggle.

The empty shape of the shelter where they had held the clothing distribution loomed ahead a little to her right. She could distinguish the silhouette of the crippled Land Rover parked by its side. Its form seemed comfortingly familiar in all the confusion.

Kurt would go to the Land Rover, she told herself. *It would feel safe.*

She looked nervously at the running shapes ahead of her. She glanced behind. No one seemed to have noticed her silent figure standing still in the darkness. She darted toward the hulk of the vehicle. Even as she reached it, she knew Kurt wasn't there. It felt isolated and abandoned. Without her family, it contained none of the comfort and security she had hoped for.

Then she saw him. The slight figure of a boy slid silently around the front fender and came toward her.

"Kurt?" she whispered. Without thinking about what

she was doing, her thumb pushed the switch on the flash-light.

The boy wasn't Kurt. His startled face blinked in the light, but he quickly recovered. He was taller than Kurt, almost as tall as she was. His face was the color of her father's strong coffee with only a little milk, and his eyes shone fiercely from under a furrowed brow. A crown of camouflaging leaves on his head made it clear that he was with the rebels and not a village child.

How can a little boy be a rebel? Keri wondered.

The muscles in his thin arm tensed beneath a long scar. There was a knife in his hand. The knife had blood on it.

Keri stared. Her mouth felt dry, and her mind tripped over the evidence that a child not even as old as she was could use a knife to hurt someone.

The boy followed her eyes, and then looked back at her. A sly grin passed over his face. He twisted the knife slowly in her direction. The knowledge of his power was in his brown eyes.

Keri wanted to scream, but her throat was dry. Only a tiny squeak came out of her mouth. The boy smirked and stepped closer.

At that moment, the sound of Kurt's bloodcurdling scream reached her from somewhere further into the vil-lage. She turned to run toward the sound, but the boy reached out and held her arm in a grip as strong as a man's. Although the village had grown silent, the sound of her brother's scream echoed on and on in her head as though it would never end.

"Let me go!" she demanded stupidly in English.

The boy dug his nails into her arm and brought the knife close to her face.

A strange man with a machine gun in his hand stepped out from behind the Land Rover.

"*Bem feito, Mfana,*" he said.

CHAPTER 6

Keri was marched toward the neatly thatched church, conscious of the boy behind her with the bloody knife. He frightened her more than any of the grown men herding people together.

A dozen rebels in ragged clothes that couldn't be called uniforms forced a crowd into the church.

"Keri!"

She heard her mother's cry. She forgot the knife behind her and bounded forward into her arms. Her mother's clasp bruised her sides, but she wanted the pain to go on forever, just as long as her mother never let go of her. Kurt clung to his father.

"I heard Kurt scream," Keri whispered.

"It's all right, Keri." Mom held her close and stroked her hair as though Keri were a little child. "He isn't hurt. He . . . he found someone who had been killed. He's very upset."

Keri looked at where her brother's face was buried in Dad's powerful shoulder. His short legs clamped around his father's waist. Both arms gripped his neck in a stranglehold. The little boy's shoulders heaved between sobs. Their father's face was close to his, whispering calming phrases amidst the chaos.

"Why are you putting them in there?" The man with the gun grabbed the arm of a villager outside the church. His broad flat nose and fleshy face would have been ugly even without his twisted scowl. "We're taking them with us." The rebels sprang to obey his orders.

"Out! Out!" The people were herded back out of the church. Everyone was forced between the huts toward the edge of the village. A few of the rebels shouted and fired guns into the air. The rest had long knives, like the boy Mfana, or machetes. The villagers cried out and scrambled to get out of the way.

The commander turned to the Andersons. He was tall for an African and seemed pleased to be able to look down on them.

"I am Commander Elias Massingue Dube," he said in Portuguese. "You have nothing to fear if you do as I say. We have liberated you." He turned back to supervise the villagers.

"The child is all right?" Pastor Makusa laid his arm on Dad's shoulder. His coat and tie were gone.

"He'll be all right," Dad explained.

"Praise be to the ancestors that the foreign visitors are safe," Chief Mbuluzi said. A heavy woman with sagging breasts was at his side. Keri didn't see the daughter who had served at the table anywhere among the prisoners. *Perhaps she got away.*

Eventually they fell into an orderly line following a track that Chief Mbuluzi said led to the vegetable gardens by the river. It was a well traveled path, but one the Land Rover could not have managed. The rebels stopped them short of the river in an open spot between the thorn trees.

"What are we waiting for?" Keri asked.

"I don't know," Dad answered, "but we will do as we are told."

The people sat closely bunched on the ground. Keri scrunched down between her parents where she could feel their warmth and closeness and smell the minty scent of her father. She wished she could make them all invisible and slip away into the bush. There was the occasional sound of a muffled sob, or a loud lamenting wail. Keri smelled fear in the tang of sweat.

She counted heads. There were thirty-eight villagers, plus her family and Pastor Makusa. Only a dozen rebels had been left to guard them. *If this were a movie, we would make a plan to overpower them*, Keri thought. But it wasn't a movie, and Keri didn't have a plan. No one seemed to be any more willing than she to risk the guns and knives.

The other rebels made trips back and forth to the village with loads of clothing and bags of grain from the houses. Two men came carrying heavy automobile tires. Mfana had a car battery on his head. He glanced at Keri and smirked.

"The Land Rover! They're stripping the Land Rover," Dad said incredulously.

Commander Dube strutted around in the green sport coat that had been presented to Chief Mbuluzi earlier. It fitted his broad shoulders better than it had the Chief's, but looked odd with his ragged shorts.

"We have no use for the car," he informed them in a cocky tone. "Too easy to spot from the air. But we can use the parts. The rest we'll blow up."

Half an hour later they heard the explosion.

The moon was up when they were ordered to stand and form a line. Dad roused Kurt. Several times he had cried out in alarm, and his father had held him close until he had fallen asleep again. He began to cry and cling as soon as he was awakened.

"I wanna go home," he pleaded. "Let's go home, Daddy, please! I don't wanna stay here!"

Keri felt the same way. She shivered and pressed her arms into her stomach. They were prisoners right along with the people they had come to help. Why had they ever thought they could make a difference? The rebels had stolen everything from these people time and again. By bringing them clothes, the Andersons had only brought them something else to be stolen. And now more had died.

Keri saw the woman who had turned away from the black silk blouse yesterday. She draped a ragged *capulana* over her head. The mother's voice rose once more in the wail Keri had heard in the night. Even in her pretty pink blouse, Keri knew she was in mourning.

"Tomé! Raphael!" Dube ordered. "You will stay behind and bury mines in the trail so we will not be followed." Two men nodded. "The rest of you, load up."

Each person was given a bundle to carry on his head.

Pastor Makusa struggled to raise a heavy tire. Two rebels mocked his weakness and helped him settle it around his neck.

"This will make a half dozen pairs of sandals, old man," one of them said.

Keri wondered what she would be given. She huddled close to her parents. Her father held Kurt firmly in his arms.

The commander stopped in front of them. "You are Americans," he said. "Americans are our friends. You should be on our side in this war, not on the side of those criminals in Maputo. I will protect you from the government."

He held out the denim backpack. "*Mulungos* are too weak to be of any use." He used a local word for "white people." He sneered when he said it as though they were something that had crawled out from under a rotten log. "You can carry this." He handed the pack to Mom. "If there is anything missing, you let me know," he called over his shoulder. "I'll kill whoever stole it." Keri didn't doubt that he meant it.

Her mother breathed deeply beside her. Slowly she slid the backpack onto her shoulders without looking inside.

&c.

They marched for the rest of the night. Keri was grateful for the moonlight. The line of prisoners bearing spoils stretched ahead and behind like the *coluna* on the day they had traveled to Chibuto. How many days ago was that? Only a week? The city of Maputo seemed as remote as a picture in her geography book, and America only something Keri had dreamed in her exhaustion. She had not slept. Every sense in her had stayed alert, ready for whatever danger might come. Now she was lulled by the rhythm of her endless footsteps, by the steady beat of feet before her and behind.

"Kurt, you are going to have to walk. I can't carry you any longer." Dad stepped out of the path in front of her, and Keri broke the rhythm of her steps to wait for him. He was all that stood between her and these violent men.

"No, Daddy! No!" Kurt gripped his father's neck as though the ground were red hot coals. His father caught his breath and hoisted his son up again.

They walked for another hour. Dad stumbled twice, and at last Kurt allowed himself to be set down. Still he clung to his father's hand.

The sun was well up when they stopped. The people dropped to the ground in the scanty shade. They piled their heavy loads beside them. The earth seemed to sway around her, and Keri lowered her head between her knees. They hadn't eaten since last night's stewed chicken. For the first time she was aware of a painful blister on her right heel.

The rebels pulled out strips of dried meat and lumps of cold porridge and began to eat. Keri's stomach grumbled. The food looked horrible, but she couldn't tear her eyes away from it. Her mouth was dry, and her head felt light.

Pastor Makusa got up slowly from his place on the ground. He approached the commander.

"The people are hungry," Keri heard him say. "They cannot go on walking without something to eat."

Commander Dube turned to look at the frightened villagers as though this were a new idea to him.

"Woman!" He pointed to Chief Mbuluzi's wife, sitting with her friends. "You will make tea." She gestured to two of the younger women and followed the commander.

They made a fire, and soon Keri was sipping hot tea from a cup she recognized as having come from the chief's own table. It was strong and sweet, and as little as it was, she felt refreshed by it.

"Dear God, thank you for what you have provided." Her father prayed over his cup as though it were a full meal. "Please give us the strength for whatever is to come, and may we bring glory to your name. Amen."

"Amen," Mom said.

Keri said nothing.

Kurt sat on his father's knee, cradling the cup in both hands and blowing on his tea.

❧

They stayed that night in an abandoned farmhouse. Its walls and floor were cement, and it must have belonged to a Portuguese at some time in the distant past. There were rusty burglar bars still on the windows. The corrugated tin roof covered only the two back rooms.

"This time the bars keep us in, instead of keeping robbers out," Keri said as she looked past them to the rebels, setting up camp and storing the bundles in the out buildings in the yard.

The Andersons were given a small bedroom to sleep in. There was no furniture—only a single reed mat rolled up in the corner. Mom unrolled it and spread it on the crumbling concrete floor. Roaches scurried to find new cover, and Mom watched them with a dazed expression. Keri stomped on the two that came near her.

"Thank you, Keri." Her mother's voice sounded faint and far away, as though it were a great effort to speak at all. Mom slipped the backpack off and looked inside. Her tired face lit with a wan smile. She pulled out a *capulana* and spread it over the prickly reeds.

"Come and sit down," she invited as she knelt on the mat. She drew out the Portuguese Bible Dad used for preaching.

"I'm glad we have that," he said.

Mom turned over the backpack and dumped the rest of the contents in front of her.

"Thank God the water filter is here," Dad murmured. "And some antiseptic cream. That will be useful." He sorted through the small pile. "Malaria medicine!" He swept up the bottle and gripped it possessively.

Mom fingered the bags of dried fruit and trail mix. "I could have brought them out when we had our tea," she apologized, looking at Dad. "But I didn't think I could do that without sharing, and . . . "

Her voice was low and miserable.

"There wouldn't have been enough to go around," Dad consoled her.

"Maybe there would have been." Kurt became more animated at the sight of food. "Remember the boy in the Bible with five loaves and two fish? Jesus made it enough to feed five thousand."

"Maybe you're right, Kurt. I'm afraid I didn't have the faith to share." Mom shook her head slowly at Dad, and Keri thought she was going to cry.

"We'd better not eat it all," Dad suggested. He knelt beside them on the mat. "We don't know how long we need to make it last."

"But I'm hungry," said Kurt.

"Elijah traveled forty days on the strength of two honey cakes and a jar of water provided by God," Dad replied. "I think we can make all this fruit and trail mix last awhile."

"We could do it like we did the M&Ms that Grandma sent for my birthday," Keri suggested. The special treat had lasted almost a month. After dinner Keri had doled out two of each color for each person, plus an extra dark brown one because there were more of them. "We could have one of each kind of fruit each day."

"That's a good idea," said Mom. She handed a dried apple slice, a dried pear half, a dried apricot, and a prune to each member of the family. Then they each had a tablespoon of peanuts, raisins, and chocolate chips for dessert.

"I'm still hungry," said Kurt quietly.

Keri didn't say anything, but she wished she had something to fill her up.

There was a knock on the door.

"Come in," said Dad automatically. The lock turned, and a young man in a tattered khaki shirt entered. He was one of those who had stayed behind to lay the mines, the one

Commander Dube had called "Tomé." He couldn't have been more than a teenager. His nostrils flared so widely that Keri could see right up into his sinuses. He wore a red necktie bound around his head like a sweatband.

"That's *Vovô Pastor's* tie," Kurt accused. Mom hushed him.

A sneer twisted the teenager's face. He held out a tin plate of porridge. It was the scrapings of the pot. "Commander Dube thought you might be hungry."

They took it thankfully.

&

As the Andersons settled themselves for the night, Keri heard movement in the corridor. From the glassless window they could see the villagers being herded into the house. There was a great deal of bumping and crying coming from across the hall.

The Andersons sat cross-legged on the mat and stared at one another.

"Are they putting everyone into the same room?" Mom asked in an awed voice. "I hope it's larger than this one," she added when no one could deny it. "Brian, there won't be enough room for everyone to sit down, much less to lie down and sleep! They must be as exhausted as we are. And will there be enough air for that many people?"

Once again Mom's eyes looked ready to spill tears. Keri wrapped her arms around her and buried her head in her shoulder. Mothers weren't supposed to cry. Keri wished there were something she could do to make it right.

The noises from across the hall echoed in the silence of their space. Keri looked up. Dad was searching the corners of their tiny room with his eyes.

"Are we prepared to share?" he asked.

No one said anything. Keri buried her face again in Mom's shoulder. Kurt stared at the pattern of the *capulana*.

She could hear Dad's shoes creak as he got up and walked to the door. He pounded deliberately on it.

"*O que é?*" a voice demanded.

"I want to speak to Commander Dube."

"*Um momento.*"

A few minutes later the door was opened, and Dad was led away. Keri had an awful feeling that they would never see him again. She wanted to pray, but no words would come except "please, please, please." She huddled beside Kurt while Mom bowed her head. No one spoke. When Dad returned, she threw herself on him in relief. He wrapped his strong arms securely around her, but his face was drawn.

"Yes, they are all in the one room. No, they will not allow us to share this space. There's a large window like this one. I think there'll be enough air." He sounded like he was trying to convince himself as much as them.

"We should try to get some sleep," Mom said. She stretched out on the mat and pulled Kurt down next to her.

"André will tell people where we are, won't he?" Keri asked as she tried to get comfortable.

"I'm sure he will. There are people praying for us right now," Dad replied.

Keri's last memory as she drifted into exhausted sleep was of her father praying aloud for Pastor Makusa and the others in the room across the hall.

CHAPTER 7

The sun was streaming through the burglar bars when Keri awoke. She knew immediately where she was, but it took a few minutes to realize why the silence frightened her so. She could hear nothing from the room across the hall. Where were the villagers? She sat up. The reeds of the mat made crinkling noises under her.

Dad turned from gazing out the barred window. He put his finger to his lips, and pointed to Kurt. The little boy was still curled on the mat breathing evenly. His shorts were damp where he had wet himself in the night. Keri wrinkled her nose at the acrid smell, and backed away, but she felt sorry for him more than disgusted.

She went to lean against her father. He popped an antacid into his mouth and draped his arm around her shoulders. Life in Africa had always been exciting, but her father had always stood between Keri and the scary parts. For the first time, she wondered if that would be enough.

"What's going to happen to us?" she asked, looking up into his face.

His hand rubbed her shoulder. He clicked his tongue thoughtfully. "I don't know," he said. His eyes, like uncurtained windows, looked directly into hers. At least she knew he would never lie to her.

"Where are the villagers?"

He looked away. Her eyes followed his gaze through the bars to where a broad path led off into the bush. There was no one in sight except for two rebels tending a three-legged iron pot on the fire.

"They were taken away early this morning. They haven't come back yet." He didn't look at Keri, and she wondered what he was thinking.

Mom stirred in the corner where she sat leaning against the wall. "Did you sleep well?"

Keri shrugged. Mom made it sound as though it were just an ordinary morning and that the whole world hadn't turned upside down in the last two days.

"We were all so exhausted," she went on, stretching and changing her position. Keri had never thought of her mother as old, but today the little lines at the corners of her eyes stood out. There were dark circles under them.

A burst of coarse laughter made her turn back to the window. The larger rebel pushed the smaller one off the log where he squatted by the fire. The two of them wrestled briefly before the boy lay submissively under his larger opponent. The victor got up and gave him a kick with another laugh before returning to the pot by the fire. The defeated rebel got to his feet and rubbed his side. He glanced toward the house, and Keri recognized the round face of the one they called simply "Mfana," "boy." She wondered what his real name was.

The young man began spooning hard porridge onto an enamel plate. He heaped it high and added something dark from a second pot. Keri's mouth watered and her stomach grumbled loudly as she imagined the taste of beans and porridge. Mfana took another plate, brushed off the sand and served himself a generous portion. He sat down out of reach of stray kicks.

Dad and Keri watched them. There was nothing better to do.

When the older soldier's plate was empty, he refilled it. Mfana started to do the same. His companion said something indistinguishable and jerked his head toward the house. Mfana looked straight at Keri. He took another enamel plate and brushed the dirt off with his hand. He heaped it with porridge and beans and headed for the house.

Keri looked hopefully at Dad.

"Breakfast?" he said. He cocked an eyebrow and smiled.

Soon they heard the soft padding of bare feet in the hall and the scrape of the lock being released. The door swung open and banged against the cement wall.

"*Comida*." Mfana thrust the plate at Dad. He held himself with pride and there was no trace of submission in his brown eyes now.

"'*Brigado*,'" Dad replied. He bowed his head in polite deference, and Mfana lifted his a little higher. Keri glared at him. Mfana never even glanced at her as he closed the door and locked it securely again.

"He's a beast," Keri murmured too low for her father to hear.

Kurt had stirred with the banging of the door. He rubbed his eyes. "Where are we?" he asked sleepily, and then his face registered remembrance. Mom moved to his side and rubbed his back.

"Good morning, Kurt," she said cheerfully. "Look at what we have to be thankful for."

They all sat cross-legged around the single plate on the *capulana*. No one said anything about the dampness. Kurt sniffed and investigated. He grimaced in shame.

Dad said grace, and they all pushed their fingers into the porridge, made little balls of it and dipped them into the beans.

"This is a lot better than slimy chicken," Keri said, trying to imitate Mom and Dad's cheerfulness.

"I wonder if *Vovô Pastor* got breakfast yet," Kurt said. Keri caught Mom and Dad looking at each other over his head. Mom looked pale, and Dad's face was grim.

"Oh." Kurt felt quickly in his pocket. "My ox!" he moaned when he had unwrapped it. One horn lay broken off in the wrapper.

Dad picked up the two pieces and fitted them together. They joined neatly, but there was no way to make them stick.

Kurt snatched them back out of his hand. "*Vovô Pastor!* He can fix it." He leaped at the door and grabbed for the handle. It was locked.

"Let me out! Let me out!" The boy pounded the door and shook the handle.

Keri sat frozen on the floor, her hand halfway to her mouth.

"Kurt! Kurt!" Dad was at his side. He gripped his shoulders firmly and pulled Kurt to him.

The little boy clung desperately to the handle. "My ox! My ox! I want *Vovô Pastor.*" His fingers slipped off the knob, and he dissolved in tears in his father's arms.

Tears were running down Mom's cheeks, too. She cried quietly without moving from her place.

Keri's throat was tight, and her face felt hot. One part of her brain insisted it was silly to cry over a homemade toy. The other part knew the tears weren't about the ox.

She heard noises from the yard. Perhaps the others were coming back. She licked her fingers quickly and wiped them on her skirt as she stood up to see.

A crowd of rebels entered the yard from the path on the far side. They laughed and jostled each other. Keri wasn't sure what it was like to be drunk, but she thought maybe they were. There were no villagers with them, only Pastor Makusa. His hands were tied, and there was blood on the side of his face. The knees of his trousers were soiled. One of the rebels pushed him ahead of them. He stumbled briefly, but somehow managed to hold himself with the same dignity Keri had seen when he preached or led in prayer.

"He's here!" she burst out. "He's all right, Kurt!"

"Where?" Kurt broke away from their father and rushed to the window. The ox was clutched tightly in his hand.

"He's hurt," Kurt whispered.

"He'll be OK. You'll see," she insisted. *He has to be, Jesus, please!* She wanted desperately for the old man to be all right, but she was too scared to say it aloud even to Jesus. More than that, she wanted Kurt to be all right. "See how tall Pastor Makusa stands."

Dad and Mom had come to stand behind them. There was a loud sob, and Mom's shoulders shook as she buried her face in Dad's chest.

"Why is Mom crying?" Kurt asked.

"She's just happy that Pastor Makusa's back," Dad replied, rubbing his wife's shoulder as he had Keri's earlier.

Keri crossed her arms and pressed them into her stomach. It would probably feel good to cry.

She turned back to the window. Commander Dube had discovered the pot of food and the dirty plates. He began shouting at Mfana and the young man and swinging the heavy corn stamper he carried like a club. He struck Mfana a blow on the shoulder. The boy dodged, but a blow on the chest brought him down.

Keri gripped the bars of their prison. The boy had frightened her. He was vicious and proud, but no one deserved to be treated that way. What she had eaten turned over in her stomach. Her heart pounded with rage. Impotence held the bitter taste of vomit.

Pastor Makusa stepped forward.

"You want to die after all?" asked one of the rebels, throwing his head back in a vicious laugh.

Another grabbed the old man's arm and held him.

The commander swung once more at Mfana and then hurled the heavy stamper into the bush. He turned back to the pot of food as though nothing had happened and filled a plate.

Mfana crawled to the base of a tree where he curled himself in a ball.

Keri glared at the men. They filled their stomachs as though a hurt child mattered no more than the corn the stamper was intended for.

The soldier who was holding Pastor Makusa's arm dropped it and joined his comrades around the fire. The old man was left alone. He moved slowly to the curled-up boy and knelt beside him.

Mom stopped crying. She wiped the tears and went back to the mat. She leaned against the wall and closed her eyes. Her spirit of adventure was gone, and she didn't look cheerful.

Keri's stomach hurt and her head throbbed. Kurt took a few more bites of beans and porridge.

"I'm full," he said, curling himself in a dusty corner of the room.

In a few minutes they again heard footsteps and voices. The door opened, and Pastor Makusa was pushed in. He rubbed the purple marks where his wrists had been untied.

"*Vovô Pastor!*" Kurt leaped to his feet and gripped the old man's legs in a bear hug. Keri stood close to him, grinning and wanting to give him the same welcome, but feeling shy. The old man reached a dark arm to draw her in, and she leaned gratefully against him. In a moment she felt Mom and Dad joining the hug. Her knees were weak with relief. Now they were really all together.

"*Vovô*, my ox broke," Kurt said quietly.

The tight group fell apart, and Kurt lifted the damaged toy for inspection.

Pastor Makusa took it gently in his fingers and turned it over. "I don't think I can fix it," he said. His head turned toward the barred window. "I will make you another one when I find the right piece of wood." He handed Kurt back the broken ox. He patted him fondly on the shoulder, but Keri saw his eyes drawn outside to the curled-up form under the tree. "There is something about that boy . . . " he murmured. "If he smiled, perhaps I would know."

"He'll never smile," Keri said, taking *Vovô's* hand and leading him to the mat.

"You should eat and then tell us the news." Dad handed the plate to the African. It was messy where they had all dipped into it, but there was still enough to "kill the beast," as the Africans said. Keri understood now why they referred to hunger as a "beast."

She wanted to ask right away where the others were, but that wasn't the African way. The visitor must share a meal first and then the news would be given. "That is in case the news is bad and no one feels like eating afterwards," Pastor Makusa had explained to her. Keri had a sick feeling in her stomach that this might be one of those times.

Pastor Makusa bowed his head and murmured his thanks to God. Then he neatly rolled little balls of porridge in his right palm with his thumb and dipped them into what remained of the beans. Keri was pretty sure he had eaten nothing but yesterday's cup of tea since the time they had been taken prisoner, but he ate as neatly as though he were an honored guest at a wedding feast.

79

When he was finished, he sucked the ends of his fingers and wiped them dry on the *capulana*.

"They roused us early this morning," he began. "You know that we spent the night in the room across the hall." They all nodded. "There are no bars like in this room. They nailed boards over the door and windows so that no one could escape. There were so many people in the room that not everyone could sit at the same time, much less lie down. We had to stand or sit in one another's laps.

"The room was stifling, without air, and women and children cried. I was the only pastor to comfort others, although I was in need of comfort myself."

He bowed his head, and Keri wondered if he would be able to go on. The blood pounded in her ears. She didn't want to hear what happened, and yet she had to know.

"When morning came, they took us from the bedroom where we were held prisoner. We continued walking toward the place where they intended to kill us. We walked for nearly an hour. They began to separate the men from the women and to beat us.

"I found myself on my knees in the middle of the road, the first designated to die. The soldiers joked that as the *Pastor*, the shepherd, I could lead the sheep into the afterlife. I asked the commander, and he permitted me to make a prayer to God. After I finished my prayer, I closed my eyes and bowed my head, prepared to meet my Lord."

Keri held her breath. Kurt leaned forward on his knees and pressed against *Vovô*'s leg.

"The commander gave orders for the execution." The

storyteller lifted clasped hands over his head. "A man raised a heavy grain stamper to split open my skull. Suddenly his arms had no strength. He could not hold the stamper." Pastor Makusa limply dropped his arms and spread his open palms.

Keri heard her mother gasp. Her brain was numb, and the sound seemed to come from very far away.

"When he tried a second time, there came a voice that said, 'This one is not to die.' He looked around to find the source, but there was no one. The strange voice repeated once more, 'This one is not to die.' Frightened, my would-be executioner kicked me aside saying, 'Get out of here.'

"I got up, and one of the men took out a knife and cut me on the head." He touched the place from which the blood had run down his face and dripped onto his white shirt. "But the commander rebuked him."

His voice grew so quiet Keri could barely hear the words she dreaded. "So they began and clubbed to death all the others."

CHAPTER 8

Keri hunched over and pressed her arms into her stomach. They were dead. The woman with the pink blouse, Chief Mbuluzi, all of them. She ought to cry, but there were no tears big enough. Grief seemed to fill every crevice of her soul like musty air in a closed room. Grief, but at the same time guilty relief. She wasn't dead. Her parents and Kurt weren't dead. And here was Pastor Makusa. They were still alive.

Keri swallowed the tight lump in her throat.

There was a silence like the whole world had stopped breathing. Mom pursed her lips. Her hand trembled as she fingered a fold in the *capulana*. Dad took an antacid from his pocket and chewed it slowly. Kurt stared at the little ox, turning it over and over in his hand. He wiggled closer to Pastor Makusa who wrapped his arm around the little boy.

"Anda! Já, já!" The door swung open in the late afternoon. Tomé held a rusty automatic. The red tie around his forehead looked like a bloody gash. He motioned for them to hurry.

Keri put on her shoes and tied them while Mom stuffed the *capulana* hurriedly into the backpack.

Soon they were walking down the same path the villagers had taken that morning. Keri willed herself to think of nothing but putting one foot in front of the other. She was glad the soldiers carried loot and not the grain stampers they had held earlier.

Kurt walked side by side with *Vovô*. Keri stepped to his other side and slipped her hand into *Vovô's* big black one. It was the rough hand of a leader who was not too proud to work the fields alongside his people. He squeezed her hand and gave her a gentle smile.

The afternoon sun cast stark shadows in the deep footprints that crowded the sandy path. A painful knot twisted in Keri's stomach long before the footprints turned aside into a thicket. The buzzing of insects filled the air. The column of rebels and prisoners passed on without turning into the thicket. Kurt peered around his father in the direction the footprints had taken, his eyes wide, the muscles of his face tense. Keri kept her face turned away. The pain in her stomach lessened, and she stepped more lightly once they passed the spot.

Kurt must have felt the relief, too. He began to chatter about the birds and trees and to ask *Vovô* when he would make a new ox to replace the one with the broken horn.

"It needs a piece with a knot in it," *Vovô* told him. "Perhaps when we stop to rest we will find one."

The sun dropped behind the thorn trees, and the tropical dusk turned quickly to night. It was long after dark when they stopped briefly to sip a cup of water and eat a lump of cold porridge.

Kurt peered into the bushes. He kicked the ground angrily. "It's too dark to find a knotty piece," he complained. "Why do we have to walk at night?" No one answered him.

Pastor Makusa nodded absently and watched the rebels. His eyes rested often on Mfana.

After the break Keri noticed her mother limping. She went to walk beside her.

"I'm all right," Mom insisted. "I'm just getting a little blister. I'll manage."

The rebels always kept a close eye on them. Sometimes Mfana walked near them. His dark skin hid the bruises of the morning's beating.

Sometimes Tomé strode near by. His skin was smooth. He couldn't be very many years older than Mfana, but his eyes were as hard as his muscles. Keri tried not to look at the flaring nostrils that threatened to suck her up into the dark cavern of his head. But her fear turned to anger every time he struck Pastor Makusa and demanded that he go faster.

"We should just kill you and be done with it!" he shouted in Portuguese. He gave the old man a vicious shove with the butt end of his weapon.

"You leave him alone!" Keri demanded. She dropped her mother's hand and rushed at the brawny young man.

From the corner of her eye she saw Pastor Makusa stumble against Kurt who struggled to hold him upright. The butt of the gun swung toward her chest. Her brain said she had to stop before she reached it, but her body had already received the order to rush. She could do nothing to hold back its momentum.

Strong arms reached under her armpits, gripped her shoulders, and lifted her off the path. Her feet kicked wildly at the air, and she screamed. She heard the gun thump against flesh, but felt no pain.

"Uff!" A loud grunt exploded above her head. Keri smelled the minty smell of her father. She stopped kicking. Slowly, Dad set her feet on the ground. He doubled over, gasping for breath and clutching his side.

She still trembled with anger, but her gut twisted with remorse. "Oh, Dad, are you OK? I'm so sorry."

"Maybe we should kill the whole lot of you!" Tomé threatened. He turned the gun so the barrel pointed toward them. His eyes gleamed white in the darkness.

"What's going on here?" Commander Dube pushed the gun aside. The column had stopped. The commander stood before them, legs astride the trail, his hands on his hips.

"The old man is too slow," a soldier complained. "Tomé thinks we should kill him and be done."

"But didn't you hear the voice of the spirit?" argued a thin man. His earlobes had long slits from a traditional initiation ceremony. "We can't kill this man!"

Murmurs of agreement rose from the group. "What would happen to us if we killed a man with such a powerful spirit?"

But Keri saw in the eyes of some that they agreed with Tomé. They would reach their destination faster without this old man slowing them down.

Dad straightened up and breathed deeply. He faced the commander squarely, saying nothing.

Commander Dube's eyes went from one to the other. He looked at the little boy standing close to the old man. He turned toward Mom whose face was streaked with sweat and dust. He looked at Keri who glared back at him. She wondered if he had heard Tomé's suggestion to kill them all. His eyes rested on Dad's for a long time as though he were wondering what kind of white man this was, how much he could get by with in his presence, and how much trouble he was worth.

"I will walk with Pastor Makusa," Dad said calmly. "Together we can keep up." Keri's heart swelled with confidence in him. Dad whispered something to Kurt as he slipped his arm under the African's.

Kurt glanced back to where his mother stood leaning forward with her head bowed and hands braced against her knees. Keri wasn't sure if she was resting or praying. Probably both. Kurt dropped *Vovô*'s hand and came to her side. Keri moved to the other and together they formed a tight group with the two men. Dad would take care of Pastor Makusa. He could take care of all of them.

"Move out," the commander ordered.

❧

The sun was well up when they stopped at a crumbling *rondavel*. They had passed nothing for hours that looked like it might be lived in.

The five prisoners were herded into the dark hut. It smelled of rotting thatch and something worse. Kurt sneezed.

Keri kicked rubbish away with her foot so Dad could lower Pastor Makusa to sit leaning against the wall. He looked very frail. Only the gleam of sweat kept his face from disappearing into the deep shadow when he closed his eyes.

"You were a trooper tonight, Kurt." Dad clapped him on the shoulder. "I was proud of the way you kept up. How are your feet, Diane?"

Mom gently untied her hiking boots and peeled off her socks. There was blood on the heels. "I hope I can keep up as well as Kurt did tonight," she said. She rummaged in the pack for the antiseptic cream and spread some on the sores.

Keri could hear the rebels lighting a fire and, after a while, a single plate of porridge was shoved through the door. At least it was warm and fresh. Keri pushed the first few bites into her mouth eagerly, not caring if her hands were washed or her manners good. But as soon as the edge had been taken off her hunger, a warm lethargy crept over her. She wanted sleep almost more than food.

"Eat something, *Vovô*," Kurt said. The pastor was still holding his first ball of porridge in his hand. He worked it gently from time to time so that it appeared that he was eating when he wasn't. Kurt took the ball of porridge and lifted it to the old man's lips. He nibbled obediently.

"I'll eat after I've slept," he promised.

Dad helped him lie on his side and coaxed him to eat a little more. Dad's voice reminded Keri of the time when she had mumps and they didn't know any doctor in Maputo.

Mom curled up on the *capulana* on the floor. She gestured for Kurt to join her.

He shook his head. "I'll stay with *Vovô*." He nestled next to the old man, his head near the black man's heart. He flung his arm over the big man's shoulders as though he could protect him.

Keri wanted to stomp through the low door of the hut, shake those evil men like naughty boys, and tell them Pastor Makusa was an old man. They were African; they should know about respecting old people. *That would do just about as much good as Kurt's arm around him*, she thought.

Her father gingerly examined his bruised side. He lowered himself a little stiffly and stretched across the entrance. "Get some sleep, sweetheart," he said.

Keri took off her shoes. Her feet felt swollen to twice their normal size. The muscles of her legs were as tight as though she were still dragging them forward over the trail. She lay down next to her mother. The ground was hard and unyielding. Her arm made an awkward pillow. When she closed her eyes, she could still see the shifting image of the path. At last she slept.

&c

When they woke in the evening, Pastor Makusa had a cheerful smile. He ate the porridge the family had left for him and drank the tea Keri brought. *He'll be all right*, she told herself.

Mom put on her shoes carefully. The blood on the socks had dried to a hard crust, which she softened in a little of the water they had been given. Brown things floated in it. Dad found the water filter in the backpack. He asked for a clean cup and carefully pumped the water through the filter from one cup to the other before he let them drink.

"It's time." The thin soldier who had argued against killing Pastor Makusa was at the door.

Mom winced when she stood up. She didn't say anything, but Keri took her hand.

"Come on, *Vovô*. I'll help you." Kurt struggled to pull the old man to his feet.

Vovô chuckled weakly. "You are a good grandson," he said. Dad led him down the path at the prodding of the rebels.

Keri saw Kurt reach into the pocket that held the wooden ox and pull it out. He must have rolled on it in his sleep; the second horn had broken off. Kurt looked after Pastor Makusa as if he were thinking of asking again when *Vovô* would make a new one. He bit his lip instead and slid the ox back into his pocket without saying a word. She followed him up the path.

They made slow progress that night. Pastor Makusa leaned heavily on Dad and couldn't go for more than an hour without a rest.

"We have to move faster!" Commander Dube raised his arm and stiffly brought it back to his chest, fist clenched, as though he had intended to strike and thought better of it. He glanced frequently at Dad. Keri wondered which he feared more, the spirits or the white man. He had sent most of the party on ahead carrying the bundles of loot and keeping only a small escort with the prisoners. Mfana was there. So was Tomé and the thin man who feared spirits.

Each rest seemed shorter than the one before, and each time Keri wondered if *Vovô* would be able to continue. The darkness pressed in around her. Who knew what might be lurking there? It could not be more evil than what walked with them.

"Pedro." The commander nodded to the thin man as they ended their third rest. Pedro approached the prisoners.

"I will help the old man." He bowed in deference and used a local term of respect. He drew one of Pastor Makusa's arms gently over his shoulder and helped him to his feet. Dad stiffened and seemed ready to refuse the offer, but he himself had stumbled twice in the last mile. He nodded slowly and slid his shoulder under Pastor Makusa's other arm. Together they raised him.

For twenty minutes they walked that way, more quickly than they had all night.

"He'll make it. You'll see," Keri told Kurt. The boy kept looking back to reassure himself that they were still following. His fingers constantly sought his right pocket with his wooden ox.

Another soldier offered to relieve Dad. He gratefully gave up his place and stretched upright for the first time in hours.

The soldier who took Dad's place was one who had been polite to them, but Keri saw a satisfied gleam in Tomé's eyes, and the hair rose on her arms.

The path wound downhill through thicker bush. The trees were larger here, their tops lost in the darkness above. Keri wondered if they were approaching a river. The way was narrow, and they walked single file. She frequently glanced behind to be sure Mom was keeping up. Although Mom limped badly when they first started, sheer determination seemed to carry her through the pain.

The numbers in their escort were fewer now, but Keri lost sight of the front and the end of the line in the darkness. When she turned around, she could see no farther than the soldier behind Mom. She could hear Kurt's voice and his and Dad's footsteps following in the darkness.

After a while, she realized that they were walking faster than they had in the last two nights. Dad must have realized it, too. She heard him arguing with the soldier behind Mom. Her father jogged around her toward the front of the line.

Around the next bend, they all came to a stop.

"They've fallen behind," Dad was explaining to Commander Dube. "We must wait for them."

Keri looked back and realized Pastor Makusa and the soldiers helping him were the only ones missing.

"We're not waiting," the commander replied. "We will camp by the river tonight. They will catch up with us there."

"I'll go back and help them," Dad said.

"You will not go back."

"You can send a soldier with me. I won't run away while you have my family. You know that." His voice rose but remained controlled.

"You will not go back. I said, they will join us at the river." Commander Dube shifted his weapon and stared into Brian Anderson's eyes without blinking.

No! We have to go back! Keri screamed inside, but she clenched her teeth and waited for her father to insist. Kurt stood beside her, holding his breath. His hand was in his right pocket where he kept the broken ox.

Dad looked from their mother to the children. He seemed to be weighing what might happen if he disobeyed. Several soldiers shifted their weapons in readiness. Dad's shoulders drooped. At that moment Keri hated him for backing down.

"You will go forward!" the commander said. His voice was full of the confidence of victory over the despised *mulungo,* the white man. He gave Dad a shove toward the river. Dad looked years older than *Vovô* as his eyes met Mom's, and he turned to obey.

CHAPTER 9

They spent the day hidden in a banana grove on the far side of the river. The shelters built from the broad leaves under the trees must have been invisible from the air. But the Andersons were never invisible to their captors. Keri found it almost impossible to do her necessary business squatting in the bush with an armed rebel a few feet away, watching.

Kurt cried himself to sleep. He clutched the tiny wooden ox in his sweaty hand and sobbed as though his heart would break. Keri was too exhausted to cry. She was asleep almost before she closed her eyes. She woke to a piercing scream. For an instant, she was back in the village on the night of the attack.

"It's all right, Kurt. It's all right." Mom quieted the boy's sobs. He must have had a nightmare. Mom softly began to sing remembered lullabies. Keri curled in a ball like a kitten and pressed her arms into her stomach, trying to pretend Mom was singing in her own room in Maputo. The cold hardness of the ground made pretending difficult. She drifted into a doze. Had Pastor Makusa arrived in camp yet? They promised. . . .

She dreamed they were going to Swaziland for a week at the hot springs. They would eat in restaurants and read library books and swim all day. They were flying in a small plane. Keri could hear the hum of the motors. Gradually the sound became more distinct. She was awake. There really was a plane, but they weren't on their way to Swaziland. They were prisoners on their way to who-knew-where.

Keri sat up quickly. Maybe the plane was looking for them. She should jump up and run into the open and wave her arms in the air. The plane would see her, and they would be saved. They would go to Swaziland, and her dream would be true.

A guard stared at her. He leaned forward, muscles tense, ready to spring if she moved. Tomé trained his weapon on Dad. Their eyes were locked as though he dared her father to attempt contact with the plane. Another soldier aimed his gun at Mom.

"Your turn." The voice of the boy, Mfana, was as calm as a child playing in the backyard. He looked at Pedro, squatting with him in the dust of a nearby shelter. The slit lobe of the man's ear almost brushed his shoulder as he cocked his head to listen to the sound of the plane.

Mfana never glanced at the sky. He shrugged at Pedro's inattention and flicked a pebble in the dirt. It appeared to be some sort of game. When Pedro still did not respond, Mfana flicked his stone again and picked up two stones with a satisfied grin on his face. It seemed to Keri that he was deliberately shutting out the motor and the tense silence of his companions. He didn't want to think about it, like her not wanting to think about what could happen that day on the *coluna*.

Commander Dube sat casually under one of the shelters. His eyes followed the sound of the search plane as if he could see it through the thick screen of banana leaves. The sound faded and grew more distant.

Kurt shifted beside her. He smelled of fresh urine. Keri wished they could take a bath. They all stank. Her heart sank into her gut while the drone of the motor faded in the distance.

The men relaxed. Keri stood up. She walked straight to Pedro. "Where's Pastor Makusa?" she demanded. "Commander Dube said he'd meet us at the river." Her voice had a hard tone she didn't recognize as her own.

Pedro shrugged. "*Sei lá.*"

"You killed him, didn't you?" she accused. Her eyes narrowed in angry slits. "After everything, you killed him just like you killed the others!"

She flew at the man and batted his head with her fists. He fell backwards from his squat and raised his arms in protection. Keri tore at him all the harder. Her father's strong arms reached around her and pulled her away. She struggled and turned her blows on him.

"They killed him, and it's all your fault!" she sobbed. "You could have saved him! You should have made them go back for him! Why didn't you protect him?" Something inside her screamed, "How do I know you'll protect the rest of us?" But she didn't say it out loud. She couldn't admit a fear so terrible, not even to herself.

"No! No!" the African insisted. "We didn't kill the *velho*. We even left him a lump of porridge and a little water." He looked horrified that Keri would think he might go against the spirits. "The Spirit who said he was not to die will take care of him. He's a very powerful spirit. I'm sure of that." The man gingerly felt the side of his forehead where Keri had struck him.

Dad made no effort to protect himself from Keri's anger. His face was gray, and his lips were drained of blood. The strength went out of Keri's arms, and they dropped limply to her sides.

"What could I do, Keri?" Dad moaned.

"You should have done something!" she sputtered. "What if we all refused to go any further, then what?"

He closed his eyes and said nothing.

❧

Keri's stomach hurt so much she could hardly eat. The rebels made a fire when they were sure the plane would not return. They cooked some of the food they had taken from the village. Keri gagged on it.

She walked with her mother that night. Mom was still limping. What if Commander Dube decided she was holding them up? What if he left her behind as well? Would Dad protect her? Or would he abandon her like Pastor Makusa?

They set a fast pace, and Keri had to trot to keep up. The moon was waning, and it was darker than last night. She tried to pray, but there was so much she couldn't put into words. All that came out was a pitiful "Help me! Help me!" in rhythm with the drumming of her feet. She tripped on a root in the blackness. She skinned her knee when she fell and bruised her hand on a rock.

"Come on, Keri, you can do it." Dad's hand reached to help her up.

"Don't you touch me, you murderer!" She batted his hand away. The shadows of the night couldn't hide the shocked pain on his face.

"Keri! Keri!" Mom knelt and wrapped her arms around her.

"*Vamos!*" Tomé's weapon poked her back and shoved her against her mother. She would have turned on him as well, but Mom's embrace tightened and held her. Slowly she relaxed.

"Get up, Keri," Mom whispered. "We have to keep going."

Keri wanted to sit in the dirt, crying and nursing her hurt knee, but she took her mother's hand and clung to it.

They loped along for several hours. When they stopped to rest under a mango tree, Keri fell instantly asleep. She dreamed of plunging into the hot spring in Swaziland. Its waters closed over her head, and her body drifted lazily in its warmth like a womb. It seemed only a moment later that she was nudged awake.

"Time to go, Keri," Mom said.

Dad had tied Kurt to his back like a giant baby. Her brother's head lolled sleepily on her father's shoulder. Keri's arms broke out in goose bumps from the chill of the night air. She shook herself awake. She forced herself to think only of Kurt's form, bouncing ahead on her father's back. Mom trotted in front of him, and Keri wondered if her father was as worried as she was that her mother would be left behind.

She could see nothing in the darkness except the dirty *capulana* that held Kurt. It seemed to be moving down a long dark tunnel infinitely far away. Millions of pin-prick stars were painted on stone walls that arched overhead and closed off any reality except the path. A soldier stumbled somewhere ahead. A ripple of laughter shattered the walls of the imaginary tunnel and jerked her awake.

"*Silêncio!*" The sharp voice of Commander Dube quieted the laughter.

For a week they traveled by night and hid by day. On the second night of the second week, the rebels slung a mat between poles and carried Mom, whose feet were so tender she could hardly stand. The knot in Keri's stomach relaxed only a little knowing her mother would not be left behind.

❧

One morning they seemed to make a wide circuit to avoid a populated area. Before it was quite light, Keri glimpsed the neat rows of a cultivated field. They ate better that evening, and Keri wondered if the villagers had brought them food. The band had been reduced to eating dried elephant tripe boiled in water with corn meal porridge. Keri wasn't sure which was worse, the smelly tripe or the maggots in the porridge. *What I wouldn't give for some slimy chicken,* she thought and wrinkled her nose.

Another morning the Andersons found a papaya by their backpack. The end was bruised from its fall. A gash marked where a rock had knocked it from the tall plant. It tasted cool and sweet.

"Eat a few of the seeds," Mom directed. "They'll help to keep you regular."

Kurt screwed up his nose.

"Eat them," Dad instructed. Both children obeyed. The little black seeds burned Keri's mouth like mild peppercorns. She scraped her papaya skin over her teeth to cool her tongue with the last of the pulp.

The morning they came upon the goat, Commander Dube declared a day's rest. They would feast. His men seemed as pleased as the children. The goat must have escaped an earlier pillaging of the area, but it didn't escape this time. Keri felt sorry for the animal, but hunger pushed pity aside. She fell asleep almost happy and woke to the smell of cooking meat.

Mom bathed her feet carefully in filtered water. "They're doing much better," she declared. "I think I'll try to walk part of the way tomorrow night." She stroked Keri's hair. "You're doing great, Keri. God will get us through this. You'll see."

Dad patted her back. She shrugged him off and gave him

a sullen look. She couldn't forget what he did to Pastor Makusa.

When Pedro brought them a plate of stewed meat and porridge, Keri's portion quickly disappeared. Her stomach didn't even hurt. Not much, anyway.

Kurt arranged eight small, oddly shaped bones in a neat double row. Mom said they were vertebrae.

"What are you doing?" Keri asked.

"They could be oxen, don't you think?" Kurt lay on his stomach in the dirt and eyed the odd bones closely. He never played with the broken ox *Vovô* had given him. It stayed in his pocket, and Keri saw him often reach inside to rub his fingers over its surface. "Oxen to pull a covered wagon," he went on. Kurt liked stories about the *voortrekkers*, the pioneers of Southern Africa, who had crossed the wilderness in covered wagons in the 1800s.

Keri smiled. The muscles of her face felt tight. They hadn't smiled in a long time. "They do look like oxen," she replied. "Too bad we don't have the jawbone." The jawbone was what the *voortrekker* children used for a wagon.

"Let's look for it." Kurt hopped to his feet and dashed off.

Keri followed him. She didn't like him to be out of her sight. What if he were left behind?

There was no single garbage heap to search. The rebels tossed their bones over their shoulders into the bush behind them as often as not. No one was concerned about keeping the campsite clean.

The rebels had grown friendlier in recent days as they

moved deeper into their own territory. Keri was pretty sure no one intended to kill them. Commander Dube seemed more concerned with convincing her father that the government in Maputo was wrong and that his side was right. If only they would let them go home. She wondered if the guards would be concerned about two prisoners wandering around the edges of the camp in the dusk. It would be so easy to slip off into the bush, easy to walk away from these men who were forcing them to march.

And then what? Where would she go? What would she eat? She would wander alone in the wilderness like the goat until the next group of rebels came along and found her. That is, unless she starved to death first.

"There it is!" Kurt pointed. The bone had been boiled clean of meat and the softer parts had been chewed, but it still looked vaguely like the runners of a miniature sled. Kurt picked it up from beside a tall clump of yellow grass and brushed off the dirt.

A few inches from where it lay was a callused, black foot about the size of Keri's own. Keri's eyes moved up the dusty, bare leg to the still face of Mfana. No doubt he was another reason why no one was concerned about their running away. He seemed to stick to them like a dark shadow.

"We're making a covered wagon," Kurt announced cheerfully. He darted back into the camp.

Mfana didn't move. He only watched Kurt with deep brown eyes that were like one-way glass, letting him look out, but no one else see in. His eyes turned back to Keri. She backed away uneasily and turned to follow her brother.

Playing with the oxen and wagon let them forget for the moment their current situation. They could pretend, instead, that they were farmers who had voluntarily braved the wilderness to seek a better life. Together they moved the oxen forward a few inches at a time, one by one, and then the wagon.

Mfana watched them silently from a log near the fire. His expression never changed. Once Keri looked up, and he was gone. Without his dark eyes on her, she took courage to return to the edge of the camp and break off seed pods that could serve as people.

"A father, a mother, a boy, and a girl," she announced, displaying her finds and positioning them in the "wagon."

"Let the boy be the biggest," Kurt demanded. "He should be big enough to have a gun and kill Zulus."

"Kurt!" For a shocked moment, Kurt's nostrils seemed to flare like Tomé's. Dad had always insisted that even in play they pretend to hunt only animals and never people.

"OK. Elephants," Kurt backed down. "But he needs a gun."

"Impala would taste better," Keri mumbled. Kurt was already moving the wagon forward one ox at a time. It was slow work moving eight oxen individually to pretend that they were pulling the wagon. Keri grew impatient.

Suddenly Mfana was there. In his hand were two long strips of grass. He dropped to his knees beside them. Silently he picked up one of the oxen and fastened it with the grass. His fingers flashed back and forth. His nails were as chewed as Keri's. He skillfully added ox after ox until he had woven each one into a double yoke and fastened the ends to the wagon.

"Hey, that's cool!" said Kurt. His eyes were fixed admiringly on the older boy.

Mfana finished and set the completed toy back in the dirt. Kurt reached for the lead pair and slowly moved it forward. The four teams and the jawbone wagon followed. They bumped neatly over the dust Kurt had smoothed into a road. His face glowed with pleasure. Keri thought she saw the hint of a smile on Mfana's face and more than a hint of pride.

"You weren't always a soldier, were you?" she whispered.

The spell was broken. Mfana looked quickly at her. Keri thought she glimpsed something like pain before his eyes became blank once more. He disappeared into the bush behind them.

CHAPTER 10

"Malaria pills today," Dad reminded them the next morning.

"Already?" Kurt complained. Keri tried to count the days. It was confusing when one exhausting night of walking blurred into the next. Each day was a fog of trying to sleep with biting ants and swarming mosquitoes. She listed in her mind the places they had stayed—the banana leaf shelter, the ravine shelter, the one that reminded her of a giant weaver nest where they had spent several days. Yes, this must be Sunday.

The plastic bottle gave a hollow sound when Dad shook out the tablets. Keri wondered how long the pills would last. Dad never smelled of mint anymore, and Keri figured his antacids must be gone. They had expected to spend two weeks in Chibuto. They had already been gone three. Without once-a-week malaria medication the chances were good that at least one of them would get the high fever and chills spread by mosquitoes. Without treatment you could die. She tossed her dose to the back of her throat and gulped water. The bitterness clung to her mouth no matter how fast she swallowed. She tried to cover the taste with a lump of cold porridge.

Dad opened the Portuguese Bible to someplace in the New Testament. They always read a few verses and prayed together after breakfast just like at home. Only it wasn't like home. A circle of rebels watched every move and listened to every word. Keri suspected her father was speaking as much to them as to his family.

Today Dad read about Lazarus dying and Jesus bringing him back to life. Why didn't Jesus just heal him or keep him from getting sick in the first place? She had always wondered that a little bit, but today it seemed almost mean to let his friends suffer when he could have stopped it.

Dad closed the Bible, and they took turns praying.

"God bless *Vovô Pastor*," Kurt said. "Help him to get home safely." He prayed the same thing every day.

Dad prayed for the end of the war and for them to be released. He also prayed for the rebel soldiers. He seemed to know them all by name. He knew who had wives and children waiting for them to come home and who had a bad cough or a wound that wouldn't heal.

"Thank you for making Mom's blisters better," Keri prayed. "Please make my stomachaches go away. Bless Kurt and help him not to have nightmares and not to wet the bed anymore. Ow!" She rubbed the place on her leg where Kurt kicked her. She hadn't meant to be mean, but he had never wet the bed at home, and it scared her.

It was Mom's turn. "Lord, please keep us healthy even though we don't have enough nourishing food." Keri agreed.

For once in her life, she wished for a big plate of vegetables—even broccoli. "Help us to be thankful for what we do have," Mom went on. "Bless the people who are trying to get us released, and please take us home soon. Amen."

"Amen," said Dad.

"Keri, would you please put the medicine back in the backpack?" Mom got up slowly. She clutched her stomach as though it might hurt as much as Keri's did sometimes. She folded the *capulana* they had been sitting on.

As always, the shelter where they had spent the day had two entrances. "So you can escape if government troops come in the front," Pedro had explained as he arranged the branches so cleverly that the shelter could hardly be distinguished from the scrubby bush above it. Keri didn't bother to remind him that if government troops came, the Andersons wouldn't be trying to escape. She crouched to crawl through the door. Mfana's startled face looked at her from the other end. His brown hand was on the backpack.

"What are you doing here?" Keri demanded. The boy dropped something and darted away. "If you stole anything, I'll get you!" Keri ran after him, shaking her fist. He had a head start on her and longer legs.

"*Mulungo! Mulungo!*" He taunted her white skin and danced around a clump of brush. When she reached it, he was gone.

"The little thief!" she muttered as she retraced her steps and lifted the denim pack. A clump of reddish-brown litchis fell behind it. They were as plump as Concord grapes, and her mouth began to water just looking at them.

"Mom! Look what I found!" She backed out of the shelter and held up the fruit.

"God's answering my prayer already," Mom said.

"It wasn't God. It was Mfana." Keri spat the words. "I thought he was stealing something."

"Mfana?" Mom counted the litchis and divided them into four portions. "I bet he was the one who brought the papaya, too. That boy needs a family so badly." She peeled a litchi with her teeth and popped it into her mouth. "Mmm. These are delicious. Kurt, find Mfana and tell him thank you."

❧

Mfana always seemed to be hanging around. It irritated Keri. Mfana scared her. He was only a little boy, and yet he wasn't a little boy at all. He often walked with Kurt on their nightly treks. Keri had to admit that Kurt walked faster and complained less when he walked with Mfana, but she kept an eye on them. She didn't trust Mfana any more than she trusted her father. She could never quite forget the look on his face or the bloody knife the first time she saw him.

One evening while they rested before beginning to march again, Keri watched the two boys with their heads together. Kurt drew the wooden ox from his pocket.

"Pastor Makusa made him for me," he explained. He held the broken toy out to Mfana. "He said I could call him *Vovô Pastor* because I remind him of his grandson." Mfana turned the ox over slowly in his hand. "His grandson's dead," Kurt said. "The armed bandits killed him."

Mfana looked at him sharply. "How do you know?"

Kurt flushed. "I mean, it was the rebels."

Keri listened and rubbed her sore feet. She tried to find a nail to chew, but they were all painfully short already. She wished she could just sleep and not go on walking. Asleep she could forget all the worry and the pain in her stomach.

"Pastor Makusa loved his grandson very much." Kurt spoke tenderly. Keri blinked her eyes several times to keep the exhausted tears from coming. Mfana nodded thoughtfully and studied the ox.

Some of the rebels stood and stretched. "Move out," Commander Dube ordered.

Kurt held out his hand for the ox. Mfana hesitated. He put the ox in Kurt's hand, slowly, without meeting his eye.

Most days Mfana brought a little gift—a manioc root to roast or some wild onions. One day he brought a piece of honeycomb wrapped in a banana leaf. It tasted better than Grandma's raspberry meringues for dessert.

Mom treated him like part of the family. Keri wasn't exactly comfortable when he ate with them, which was most of the time now, but he had never been far away. It didn't seem to make much difference if he sat down with them or lurked on the edge listening to everything they said. He still called her "*mulungo*" but not in front of her mother. Keri didn't give him the satisfaction of seeing how angry it made her.

"Dube hinted at negotiations for our release," Dad said one evening. They had been in this same camp for three days. "He implied they might release us in Zimbabwe soon."

"Zimbabwe?" Mom asked. "How far is that?"

"I'm not sure," said Dad. "The border's in the mountains to the northwest. From the position of the sun, I would say we have been heading pretty much straight north from the beginning."

"I don't see any mountains," said Kurt. "It must be far."

Dad looked at Mfana as though he might tell them something. The boy stuck his fingers in the porridge and tripe he shared with Kurt and Keri and said nothing. Keri kept eating. Mfana never stopped until the plate was empty. If she or Kurt hesitated, they wouldn't get their share.

"Let's play *Bom Kidi*," said Mfana when the plate was wiped clean. He picked up several small pebbles.

"What's that?" asked Kurt.

Mfana looked at him blankly. "*Bom Kidi*. You know."

"Is it a game?"

Mfana scowled at Keri. "*Mulungos*." He led them to a clear space a few yards away and smoothed the dust. Mfana directed Kurt to search for more pebbles while he drew a circle two hand spans across.

"Here, Keri. Here's one for you." Kurt handed Keri a piece of pink granite.

Mfana paced off five steps from the circle and drew the starting line. He set his stone behind the line and flicked it with his finger. It leaped several inches forward.

"Like Tiddly Winks," said Kurt. "Grandma plays that."

This must be the game Mfana and Pedro were playing the day the plane came looking for us, Keri thought. It seemed like a very long time ago.

Kurt placed his stone behind the line and flicked it. "Ow!" The stone rolled over, and Kurt rubbed his finger. "That doesn't count. I want to go again."

"You," said Mfana. He pointed to Keri.

"Me?" He didn't call her *mulungo*.

"Your turn."

Keri knelt in the dust and flicked her stone. It went several inches toward the circle. Mfana smiled.

"I want another turn. It's not fair," Kurt whined.

Mfana took his turn. "Now you," he said to Kurt.

Kurt shut up and took his turn. This time he did better. They played for several minutes. When Mfana was the first to reach the goal, he claimed Kurt and Keri's pebbles, and they had to find others. They played again. And again.

"I'm tired of this." Keri sat down with her back against a tree.

Mfana's pile of pebbles was impressive. "Let's play again," he said to Kurt.

"One more time," said Kurt. "I'm gonna beat you this time." They played three more times.

"Zimbabwe's where we went to the big waterfall and explored that ancient city, isn't it?" Kurt asked Keri as he handed his sixth pebble to Mfana.

Keri nodded. "Victoria Falls and Great Zimbabwe."

"I've been to Zimbabwe lots of times," Mfana said. Keri was surprised to hear him brag. He almost never volunteered information. "Sometimes we get supplies there. There's a trail over the mountains that the border patrols don't know about. I went with Tomé once. Another time we went all the way to Mutare to bring back a man with guns."

Keri suspected that "lots of times" meant those two, but if Mfana had been there even once maybe he could show them the way. She looked around. There were always rebels within hearing distance of her parents listening to everything they said. A couple even understood English so they had no way of planning secrets. But the children were left pretty much alone.

"Mfana, we could run away!" she whispered. "You could show us the path, and we could escape to Zimbabwe."

The boy wrinkled his brow. "Why would we do that?"

"To go home!" Keri insisted. "We could go back to Maputo, and you could find your family."

"Maputo's a bad place where the evil government is." Mfana added Kurt's pebble to his pile. "I wouldn't want to go there."

"No, it isn't," said Keri. "That's just what Commander Dube says because he's a bandit."

"He's a freedom fighter," Mfana insisted. "The evil government would shoot me because I'm a freedom fighter, too." He held his head high and looked as proud as the first day Keri had seen him.

"No, you aren't," Keri said. "You're all thieves and murderers."

Mfana shifted his weight. He didn't look quite so confident.

"Don't you want to go home to your family?" Keri pushed him.

"I don't have any family." The boy rolled his pebble in his hand.

"You must have had some kind of family," Keri said. "What happened to them?"

For a moment his eyes softened, and Keri thought the shutters he kept on them might open just a crack and let her see in. He shook himself as if to brush away a bad dream.

"They're all dead," he said. He paced off five steps from the circle and positioned his pebble for the game.

❧

The next night they moved out. As she stumbled along in the dark, Keri told herself that perhaps when the sun came up she would see the mountains of Zimbabwe rising to the west, but each morning there was only more of the vast African plain.

They marched for three more nights. Each time they rested the boys played *Bom Kidi* or built *colunas* in the dirt. Sometimes Keri played *Bom Kidi* with them. She never played *coluna*. Sometimes the boys slipped away, and Keri couldn't find them. Those times it was Pedro who followed Keri like a shadow.

"Are we going to Zimbabwe?" Keri asked Pedro. She added a small branch to the bundle of firewood she was gathering.

"I can't say." Pedro shook his head and his long earlobes with the slits wiggled. "I follow orders."

"Humph," said Keri, "like when you left Pastor Makusa behind."

Pedro gave her a wary look and moved a few steps to pick up a branch. "That one have powerful spirit. You will see."

Keri's bundle wasn't heavy as much as awkward. Pedro helped her tie it tightly with a long piece of grass. Keri wished she knew how to do that herself. She wished she knew where Kurt was. She wished a lot of things. There was a dull throbbing behind her eyes.

"Uh, uh, uh, uh, uh!" Keri looked up at the sound of Kurt's voice. It came from the far side of a lichen-covered boulder. She followed the sound.

Kurt stood with his feet planted widely. He gripped a forked branch shaped uncomfortably like the Russian automatic that Tomé carried so carelessly. An elaborately prepared string of miniature vehicles wound past the boulder and around a nearby guava tree. Broad leaves and slabs of bark were loaded with seeds and pebbles collected from the bush. Some were crowded with twig people. The boy's voice erupted again in the rapid imitation of repeating gunfire. His makeshift weapon was aimed, not at the bush and the threatening bandits, but at the *coluna*.

Mfana held an armload of fallen guavas. He hurled them at the vehicles. One ripe fruit smashed into the ox cart that led the procession. It exploded and left pink bits of guava clinging to the prongs of the jawbone. Seeds and pulp mingled with the tumbled oxen.

"Cool!" cried Kurt. "Let me throw grenades. You can use my machine gun." He thrust the twisted branch at Mfana and swept up two fists full of small hard fruit from the

113

ground. Mfana narrowed his eyes. He curled his lip in an expression fit for Tomé and aimed deliberately at the *coluna*.

"Bam! Bam!" Kurt shouted. He jumped up and down with glee when he scored a direct hit. A curved length of bark flipped over, scattering twigs in the path. "I hit the bus!" Kurt yelled.

Keri's feet were glued to the dirt. She could hear the blood pounding in her ears and her heart thumping against her chest. Her bundle of branches slid to the ground. Her stomach twisted in pain.

Pedro stood patiently by her side. The concerned look on his face said that he sensed she was upset, but he didn't seem to understand why. "They are boys," he said. "They will fight. *Vamos*." He touched her arm and pulled her toward the camp.

Mfana must have heard them. He looked up. There was nothing of the little boy in his eyes—only the hardened soldier. Slowly he raised his play weapon and aimed it directly at Keri's face. There was no hint of play about him. His eyes burned into her own as though they could do what an imaginary gun could not.

Keri turned and fled.

The boys brought guavas for dinner that day. Only a few were wormy, but Keri couldn't eat them.

CHAPTER 11

Life was an endless cycle of walking, sleeping, and forcing down the nauseating food. Keri would have lost track of the days completely if Dad hadn't periodically announced it was Sunday and time for the malaria medication. On the fourth Sunday they stopped at a camp at the top of a deep ravine.

"We'll stay here for a few days," Commander Dube announced.

There were already soldiers in the camp. They were met by sentries and had to give a password before they were allowed in. The shelters were much like others they had stayed in, but a few had sheets of plastic over them, and one near the bottom of the ravine used pieces of roofing tin. It was covered with branches to disguise it from the air. That was where Commander Dube stayed. It had a clear space like a parade ground in front of it and a table where Dad was called every day to listen to political arguments and all the reasons why America should support the rebels. It was cool in the shadows of the ravine, but in the early morning or evening it was pleasant to sit in the sunshine at the top.

The second day Pedro came and collected their dirty clothes, giving them clean ones from the bundles the rebels carried. "I will see that these are washed," he said. He had done this several times along the way. He brought them water for bathing as well, but Keri never felt quite clean without soap. Her hair was a matted mess and the smell of urine never seemed to be far from Kurt.

"We can do the wash," Mom offered. Mom had never been enthusiastic about washing things by hand, but Keri suspected she wanted something to occupy her time.

Pedro looked horrified. "No! No, we'll take care of it."

"There may be people near," Dad murmured. "They don't want us to be seen."

Mom sighed. "Perhaps we should do some school."

"School?" cried Kurt. "We don't have any books or paper."

"So you can practice your arithmetic tables in your head and write the harder problems in the dirt." Mom seemed to be warming to the idea. "Keri, while I do arithmetic with Kurt, you may prepare an oral composition." Her eyes strayed toward Tomé building a fire to prepare the meal. "I'd like you to explain the steps in the preparation of corn porridge."

Keri thought of protesting, but the idea of school seemed comfortably normal. A grass mat under a scrubby thorn tree wasn't anything like their schoolroom in the garage in Maputo. There were no desks and no blackboard painted on the wall. They had no books except the Portuguese Bible that had been in their backpack. Mom made them practice reading from it, answer comprehension questions, and tell the main idea of a paragraph. Keri had to identify the parts of speech and learn spelling words in both English and Portuguese. Kurt had easy spelling words and practiced writing sentences in the dust.

"Kurt, read verse one," Mom said.

"*O senhor é o meu pastor.*"

Keri stared off into space while her brother read hesitantly from Psalm 23. *If the Lord's our shepherd, why doesn't he take better care of us?*

Soldiers came and went from the camp. It was still hard for Keri to think of them as anything more than bandits. They were all barefoot except for the few who had sandals made from the tires of the Land Rover. Their feet were as tough as leather. Most wore scraps of clothing in khaki or camouflage shades, but no two were dressed alike. Pedro strolled by, resting his arms on a rifle slung across his shoulders like a walking stick. He smiled and waved at Keri.

Mfana sat a few feet away watching and listening. Mom had invited him to join their school, but he refused. *Who takes care of him?* Keri wondered. Probably no one.

"Keri," Mom asked in Portuguese, "what is the main idea of this psalm?"

"That God takes care of us." She hadn't been listening, but she had memorized the psalm in Sunday school when she was Kurt's age. She knew that was the right answer even though she wasn't sure she believed it anymore. She wished she did.

117

After class, they played *Bom Kidi* with Mfana. They climbed into the sunshine at the top of the ravine and wandered beyond where the clean clothes were drying on bushes near camp. Mfana reached into the pocket of his ragged shorts and pulled out his hoard of pebbles from the last time.

"Me first," said Kurt, picking up a stone from the ground. Mfana's stone went only a little beyond Kurt's. Kurt was getting better. He practiced almost as much as Mfana. No one played as much as Mfana.

"That's on the line," Kurt said. Mfana measured a hand span from the circle and replaced his pebble.

Keri took her turn. Her stone dribbled a few inches and stopped far behind the others.

Kurt pranced up and down when he flicked his pebble into the circle ahead of Mfana's. "I won!" he shouted.

Keri handed him her stone and turned to Mfana with her hands on her hips. "Beaten by a *mulungo!*"

Mfana didn't look up. He had a new stone ready at the starting line.

As usual, Keri was the first to tire of the game. It seemed like the boys never stopped. They took turns for several minutes. A dull droning sound seemed to grow beyond the acacias at the edge of camp.

"No fair," came Kurt's voice.

"Hush," Keri said. "Listen." It sounded like a motor.

"It's just an airplane." Kurt eyed the circle and flicked his pebble.

"What's an airplane doing out here?" Keri asked. "Do you think they're still looking for us?" Kurt looked up.

The sound grew louder. Soldiers grabbed the clothes from the bushes and dashed for the shelters in the ravine. Two stamped out the fire where they had been brewing tea and scattered the ashes. Mfana flicked his pebble and motioned for Kurt to take his turn. Kurt's landed two inches shy.

"There isn't any airport for hundreds of miles," Keri insisted. She gnawed at the stump of a fingernail.

Kurt fumbled in his pocket and looked uncertain.

"Your turn." Mfana nudged Kurt.

"Maybe we could flag them down and get help." Keri stood up and raised her arms ready to signal. There was no one but Mfana near enough to stop her, and he seemed to be deliberately deaf.

"It's your turn, Kurt." Mfana sounded impatient.

The noise was loud and very near. Two green helicopters came into sight. The government insignia was painted clearly on their sides. They were on a course that would take them about a mile to the north of the camp. Keri began to run and wave. At that moment machine-gun fire burst from the front of the helicopters. Dust and torn leaves filled the air ahead of their path. Keri stopped short. Fear squeezed her chest until it hurt to breathe. Kurt jerked as though stung.

"They're shooting!" Keri shouted incredulously.

"Why are they shooting at us?" Kurt's face was white and tight with fear.

"C'mon!" Keri grabbed his hand and darted away from the camp, away from the helicopters. Shouts and cries rang out behind them. Fear washed over Keri like a wave that would drown her.

"Mfana!" Kurt shouted. He tugged on Keri's hand as though he would turn back. She jerked him forward. He stumbled against her legs. She couldn't do anything about Mfana, but she had to protect Kurt.

"Mfana!" Kurt called again.

A tall anthill surrounded by shrubbery offered no real protection, but Keri dragged her brother behind it. The children crouched down and let the leaves close over their heads.

"Even though I walk through the valley of the shadow of death," Keri murmured to herself. Psalm 23 said that, and then the part about not being afraid. But Keri was desperately afraid. She didn't think she had been so afraid since the night they had been captured.

She looked back the way they had come. Mfana was still crouched on the ground. Once he looked up as though wondering where they had gone. The smell of burnt gunpowder filled the air, and the helicopters turned and passed closer to camp, but the boy did not seem to notice. He returned to flicking his pebble toward the circle.

"Mfana! Get out of there!" Keri shouted. Kurt fumbled beside her and drew a lump of wood from his right pocket. It took a moment for Keri to recognize the form of an ox. Its horns and two legs were broken off. Kurt's fingers worked back and forth over its smooth surface.

"Please help us, Jesus!" Kurt prayed. "Don't let Mfana get killed!" Had it occurred to him that they could be killed as well?

Mfana stood up and looked around. "I won." He seemed about to call them to play again when a fresh burst of gunfire split the air. He gazed at the helicopters as though noticing them for the first time. They slowly banked far to the west. Evidently they didn't really know where the camp was. It was a good thing the laundry had all been brought in and the fires stamped out so quickly. The disguised shelters left no clue to be seen from the air.

A breeze blew the cold sweat on Keri's forehead. A piece of cloth fluttered under a bush. The breeze grew stronger and spread the *capulana* from Mom's backpack like a banner on the ground. It must have blown off the bush earlier and been missed in the rush to gather clothes. Keri glanced nervously toward the helicopters.

"Mfana!" Kurt called. The boy hunched low and darted toward them.

"Mfana, the cloth!" Keri pointed to the bright colors fluttering on the ground. Mfana paused. He looked at Kurt, then he looked where Keri pointed. The helicopters approached. He leapt on the *capulana* and dragged himself under a bush. The bright colors were completely covered by his brown body.

Machine-gun fire raked the ground just beyond the ravine. Keri's eyes followed the path of spewing dust and leaves. Kurt buried his head in her stomach, and she arched her body over him.

The helicopters flew off to the west. Keri gripped her brother's trembling body and waited for them to bank and return. This time they would surely pass directly over the

121

camp. The brush shelters would provide no protection from bullets. But slowly the roar of motors receded. Keri looked up to see the helicopters miles away. Occasionally she heard a burst of machine-gun fire, but she could no longer see the dust where it hit.

They waited until the planes disappeared from view. Slowly Mfana stood up and walked toward them. The *capulana* was clutched to his chest, and his eyes were still on the distant horizon.

"What on earth were you doing?" demanded Keri, grabbing the *capulana*. She could hardly stand for pain. She clutched the cloth like a child's blanket and buried her fists in her stomach. If only she could squash the knives in her gut.

Mfana was breathing hard. He shrugged. "I won the game," he said as though it made perfect sense.

"Kurt! Keri!" Mom burst from the shelters like a gunshot. Her hair blew wildly around her face. Dad was close behind her.

"Here!" Keri waved. Her knees trembled, too weak to run. The dust on Kurt's shorts had turned to mud and a wet streak ran down his leg.

"Keri! Kurt! They wouldn't let us come for you!" Mom's voice trembled. Her whole body shook like thin branches in the wind. "I was so afraid of losing you!" Mom swept them both into her arms.

Dad gripped Keri as if he would squeeze the life out of her. She felt his heart thumping against his chest. For once she didn't push him away.

"We were scared, too," said Kurt. "But not Mfana. He's not scared of anything. He got the *capulana*!"

Commander Dube strode toward them. He ripped the *capulana* from Keri's grasp and shook it in her face. "Did you think you could flag them down?" he demanded. "Did you think they would rescue you? Fool! They would have killed you quicker than any of us."

"Those were government planes," Dad replied. "They had the air force insignia. You are the ones at war, not us."

"Yes, the criminal government fights us. Wouldn't they be pleased to have you die in our hands?" The faint color drained from Mom's face. The commander squinted at him and waved an angry finger at Dad. "Do you think they care about you? The whole world knows you are our prisoners. If you die, it will make us look bad. That's all they care about."

Keri thought she would be sick. Her knees gave way, and she lowered herself to the ground. Just when she began to trust the rebels not to kill them, the government tried. If she couldn't trust the government, who could she trust? Certainly not her father who had abandoned Pastor Makusa. Not God who let all these terrible things happen. She leaned against her mother and didn't think she could move. The pain in her stomach was almost more than she could bear. Mom stroked her arm, but her fingers were icy and her eyes were a million miles away.

"*Vamos*, Kurt." Mfana knelt and drew a circle in the dust. He had a stone ready in his hand.

CHAPTER 12

They left before it was dark and walked for seventeen nights without a break. Mom had to be carried on a mat slung between poles. She was very thin. Dad followed the litter with a worried look.

Keri fell asleep along the path on the fifth night and only woke up two hours later because her father and Tomé came back to find her. After that, the rebels made a second litter, and she and Kurt took turns walking and being carried. When they finally stopped, Keri thought they must be in one of those places left blank on the big map of Africa in Dad's office—so isolated that no one had ever been there to map it.

For a day and a night, Keri slept. When she woke, the neat little shelter Pedro had built them under a tree was empty except for the denim pack and Kurt, sprawled on his back on a mat.

She slipped from the hut. A girl was coming out of a fresh bamboo enclosure. She looked like she was somewhere between Kurt and Keri in age. Vapor rose from the empty water tin swinging in her hand.

She smiled shyly when she saw Keri. "*O banho está pronto.*"

Keri wasn't sure which shocked her more—a girl in this remote place or the fact that she spoke Portuguese.

Mom rested on a mat by a cook fire. She smelled fresh and clean. "So you're awake," she said. "Hurry now. The water's hot—and there's soap! Dad put fresh clothes in the bath house for you."

Keri wanted to ask if her mother was all right, but the words wouldn't come. She was afraid of what the answer might be. It was better not to know.

In the enclosure, Keri found a skirt and blouse laid across a simple wooden bench. Beside it was a pavement of flat stones and a homemade table that held a tin can, a steaming basin of water, and a plate of soft, gray soap.

Keri stripped off her dirty clothes and stepped onto the pavement. She filled the can with water and poured it slowly over her head. The side was dented, but the sharp edges had been carefully smoothed away. Warm water rippled deliciously over her body. Muddy rivulets ran down her chest and splashed on her feet.

Keri wrinkled her nose. "Boy, am I dirty!" She quickly poured another can. When she was wet all over, she dipped her fingers in the soap and rubbed it on her body. The soap was gritty with wood ash but lathered nicely. She put a little on her matted hair.

She scrubbed her feet with sand. They were sore and tired. If they stayed here awhile, she would go barefoot and save her shoes for the next trek. They wouldn't last much longer. Her toes stuck through the canvas, and the laces were nearly worn through.

She rinsed, then laid the basin against her chest and poured the last of the water slowly over her, looking up into the blue sky and savoring every moment. She dried with a clean *capulana* and dressed in the skirt and blouse.

She emerged from the enclosure carrying her dirty things. The girl was whirling a thick stick in a grinding bowl near an African woman who rhythmically stamped corn. Mom picked stones and leaves from a large flat basket of beans. If only she weren't so thin.

The girl left her grinding bowl and came to meet Keri.

"Keri, this is Leila and her mother, *Mamani* Argentina. *Mamani* Argentina is married to Commander Dube." Mom nodded at the commander who approached them across an open space. Keri hardly recognized him. He wore a broad smile and clutched a tiny girl who giggled infectiously and patted his head with her small hand.

Commander Dube laughed himself. It was a sound Keri had not heard from him before. The child twisted in his arms and saw Leila. She wiggled down and held out a dry corncob and a rag.

"*Faz nenê!*" She toddled to the older girl and bent at the waist so that her thin back made a flat table.

Leila laughed as she knelt beside the child. "This is Sarita," she explained. She laid the corncob on Sarita's back and tied it with the rag exactly as a mother would tie her baby on her back.

Sarita stood up. Eight tiny white teeth showed in her dark face when she smiled. "*Não chore, nenê.*" She jiggled gently and looked over her shoulder at her makeshift doll.

Keri was enchanted. "She's darling!"

Commander Dube smiled benignly. "I have sent a runner to headquarters to inquire about the negotiations," he informed Dad. The two men wandered away talking.

"I'll wash," offered Leila, reaching for Keri's clothes.

"Can I help?" Keri asked.

Leila looked at her mother who glanced at Commander Dube. "If you stay at the top of the stream and don't go near the others. Remember what the commander said," Mamani Argentina replied.

Leila nodded and grabbed a battered basin similar to the one Keri had used for bathing.

"Take Sarita," her mother added.

"*Vem cá.*" Leila strapped the toddler to her back with a ragged strip of cloth. "*Vamos.*"

Keri picked up her clothes and followed her new friend past the other huts of the camp and into the bush. "Why does your mother call your father 'the commander'?" she couldn't resist asking.

"He isn't my father," Leila explained. "My mother and I were kidnapped from the north when I was Sarita's age." Sarita walked her doll over Leila's shoulders. "I don't remember very much. My real father and my older brothers and sisters are in Lomweland." Her voice was matter-of-fact. She might have been explaining that her family had moved from one city to another when her father changed jobs. "Commander Dube needed a wife," Leila went on. "Tomé's mother had died."

Keri stopped still. "Tomé is Commander Dube's son?"

Leila nodded. "I have two half brothers in the village. They're small, and Mamani won't let them come here to the camp. She doesn't want them to grow up like Tomé."

Keri couldn't blame her. "Where's the village?" she asked as they continued along the path.

"That way." Leila pointed to the east. "I'm not allowed to take you there. No one is supposed to know you're here. Commander Dube is proud that I speak Portuguese, and he thought it would be a good chance for me to practice."

"How did you learn?" Keri asked.

"*Mamani* taught me. She says there are real schools in Lomweland with teachers and books. When the war is over and we can go home, I'll go to school. My older brother José was the smartest one in his class. That's what *Mamani* says." She smiled proudly. "There aren't any schools here, but I can write my name."

"My mom teaches us," Keri explained. "Maybe you can go to school with us while we're here."

Leila's eyes grew wide, and she nearly dropped the basin. "Could I?"

"*Nenê!*" cried Sarita. Keri picked up the corncob "baby," which had fallen in the dust of the path, and restored her to her "mother." Sarita buried her head shyly in Leila's neck.

"Here we are," said Leila. She squatted down to slide Sarita off her back.

A shallow stream trickled over rocks. Tomé filled a water jug in a small pool. He sneered at Keri. His nostrils flared menacingly. Leila ignored him, and Keri was ashamed at her feeling of relief that the younger girl was between her and the rebel.

"It's better near the village," Leila apologized, "but here we won't be seen." She filled her basin with water and pushed the dirty clothes down into it.

Sarita gave her baby a bath while the girls swished the clothes in the water and soaped them one by one on a board that had been brought there for the purpose. Mfana brought Kurt's clothes, and the girls washed them, too.

Keri could almost imagine she was back in Chibuto with Pastor Makusa's granddaughter, Rute. None of the horrors of the last weeks had really happened. There were no village raids or *coluna* attacks, no kidnappings or murders. Little boys didn't carry knives, and fathers didn't abandon old men to die in the wilderness. Soon her mother would be well and strong, and they would go home.

"The Lord is my shepherd," Keri reminded herself. "Everything will be all right."

They stayed longer at that camp than they had at any of the others. Whether Commander Dube felt safer so far from the beaten path, or he was reluctant to leave his family, Keri didn't know. He seemed nicer somehow. He kept Sarita with him whenever he wasn't working and frequently disappeared in the direction of the village where Leila had said her little brothers lived.

Mamani Argentina cooked for them, and the food was better than they had had in weeks. She made enough herbal tea to drown in, but it seemed to help. By the time they had been there a few days, Mom felt strong enough to begin school.

Leila joined them and made quick progress. She was soon reading almost as well as Kurt. She came often to practice with the Portuguese Bible.

"I want to read as well as my brother José," she explained to Keri. "My real papa will be very proud when he sees me."

Mfana continued to sit on the side and watch, but Keri was sure he was listening. Once she caught him intently tracing letters in the dirt—D, M, M, D. He quickly wiped them out when he saw her watching. Keri couldn't decide if she was afraid *of* him or *for* him.

The only way that Leila had time for school was for Keri to help with the chores. Mom was too weak to help. Keri had never volunteered for housework at home, but at least she knew how to make beds and dust and run the vacuum. Stamping corn and winnowing and carrying water were a lot more work. No matter how hard she tried, Keri was about as much help as Sarita. Leila never complained, but Keri could see that she wondered how anyone could get to be thirteen years old and still not be able to carry a five-gallon container of water on her head. By age thirteen African girls were thinking about getting married.

"It's not my fault I don't know how to do this," Keri grumbled at the spring. She was tired of working so hard, tired of walking and living in the bush, tired of being afraid all the time.

"At home the water comes in pipes to your house," she explained to Leila as they waited for the containers to fill.

That was only true because they lived on the first floor and had their own storage tanks and pump. Lots of people in Maputo had to carry water up flights and flights of stairs to their apartments because the pressure was so low.

"*Não chore, nenê.*"

"Hold still, Sarita!" Leila tied the newly washed corncob doll to her little sister's back and helped her fill a hollow gourd. The child held very still and gripped the gourd of water on her head.

Keri pulled her container from the flow of water. She was determined to carry more than yesterday.

"Are you sure you want that much?" Leila asked.

"Yes, I want that much!" Keri snapped. Leila looked politely at the ground as she reached to lift Keri's tin.

"I'll do it myself." Keri jerked away, and the tin tumbled to the ground, splashing them all. She used an English word she knew her parents wouldn't like and slapped her leg. "Stupid! Stupid!"

Leila knelt and examined a large dent in the side of the tin. "It's all right," she said. "We can beat it into shape again."

"*Não chore.*" Sarita patted Keri's leg. The little girl's pigtails stood up brightly, but her small face was twisted in concern.

"I'm not crying." Keri was determined not to. She was afraid if she started she might never stop.

Together the girls refilled Keri's container, not quite so full as it had been before. Leila helped Keri lift it onto a twist of rag on her head. When Leila had arranged her own water tin, she led the way up the path.

131

"I can do this; I can do this," Keri muttered behind Sarita. They were almost in sight of the camp when she heard the soft padding of bare footsteps following her. A stifled giggle reached her ear. She knew that voice.

Holding firmly to the heavy tin on her head, she turned slowly to glare at her brother. Instantly she felt the heat rise in her cheeks. Mfana held his hands over his head miming Keri holding the kerosene tin. He lurched drunkenly from side to side. Kurt clapped both hands over his laughing mouth.

Keri glared at her brother. "Leave me alone!" she shouted in English. Mfana stared at her. He might not understand the words, but her tone was clear.

Kurt laughed loudly and danced a foolish dance. His imitation of Keri's water carrying was more ridiculous than Mfana's.

"I'm not paying any attention," Keri muttered. She turned deliberately. Leila and Sarita were almost out of sight around a clump of brush. Keri's arms ached from holding them over her head, and the weight of the water pressed down through the rag. She could feel the precarious balance as water slapped heavily against the walls of the tin. There was an uncomfortable lump in her throat and stinging behind her eyes.

Kurt jostled her arm and cool water spilled over her as he dashed around and pranced ahead.

"Kurt! Cut it out!"

Mfana followed him and danced lightly on his bare feet as he mocked her. *"Mulungo! Mulungo!"*

"*Mulungo!*" Kurt chanted with him. He seemed to have forgotten that "*mulungo*" meant "white man" and described him as much as Keri.

"*Mulungo* baby!" Kurt called. "Even Sarita can carry water better than you!"

Something exploded inside of Keri. It boiled up and burst through all the barriers she had held so long against it. She rushed at them both and hurled the water tin in their faces.

"At least I don't wet the bed every night!" she shouted. The falling tin banged against her feet and almost tripped her. Kurt's cheeks fell slack, and his blue eyes filled with pain. He didn't cry anymore in the daytime, but his sleep was full of nightmares, and every morning the mat was wet. Keri wished she could take back the words. Mfana and Leila couldn't possibly have understood her English, but she felt like she had betrayed him.

She kicked the tin aside and fled up the path in tears. She heard Sarita's startled cry as she rushed past. Her head ached, and she gripped her stomach where the sharp cramp had returned.

"I want to go home," she sobbed. She wasn't sure if she meant Maputo or Minnesota, but she knew it was someplace far from here, someplace safe and familiar and not full of strangers who frightened her and expected her to know how to do things she'd never done before.

"I just want to go home," she repeated.

There was no one outside their shelter when Keri hurled herself through the opening. She sank into the shadows and laid her head on a rolled up sleeping mat that smelled of dust and straw and mold. She cried all the tears that had not come since the day they had been taken. She cried for the father she couldn't trust anymore and for her mother who was so sick.

She cried for Pastor Makusa and for his grandson Dzumisana. She cried for the woman in the pink blouse and the one in the orange *capulana* and for all the babies and little children who were lost or hungry or scared like she was. She cried until the tears would come no more, and then she slept.

CHAPTER 13

Sarita was sick. She didn't come with the girls to get water. She didn't toddle around after Commander Dube in the camp. She stayed tied to *Mamani* Argentina's back, her cheek nestled on her mother's shoulder, the corncob clutched in her thin arm.

Leila hurried through the chores. Keri helped as much as she could in her clumsy way. They stayed near *Mamani* Argentina and only did a little reading in the Portuguese Bible for lessons.

"It's malaria," said Mom the second morning while she cut up a lemon in a kettle of hot water to pretend it was tea. "Sarita has malaria. *Mamani* Argentina was up with her all night. Even Commander Dube is concerned. I've never seen him so upset since the day the helicopters came so near the camp."

"He has a soft spot for that little one," Dad said. "There's something about fathers and little girls. . . . " He looked at Keri. She looked away until he sighed and turned back to rolling the sleeping mats. Then she watched his strong shoulders out of the corner of her eye and longed to lean against them again.

"The fever comes and goes, higher every time," Mom said. She carefully filled the mugs with lemon water and set the kettle at the edge of the fire. She folded her hands in her lap. "We have the only medication in camp."

Keri looked sharply at her mother. There wasn't very much left in the bottle. On Sunday, they had talked about trusting God when the pills ran out. A treatment required a lot more than just one pill.

Dad put a hand on Mom's shoulder. "How sick is she?"

"She's so small and undernourished!" Mom said. Tears glistened on her cheeks. "Even if she's not in danger now, the next cycle of fever could carry her off."

Dad looked old and pale.

Keri stood up and went into the hut. She came out and thrust the backpack into her father's hands. She didn't trust herself to speak. He looked hungrily into her eyes before he fished the bottle from the bag. It wasn't hard to find. The trail mix and dried fruit were long gone. The antiseptic cream had been used up. There was nothing left in the pack except the water filter and the Bible.

He opened the bottle and spilled the white tablets into his hand. "Four," he said. "Not enough to treat an adult." He studied Mom. "It isn't quite a child's dose either, but Sarita's very small. It might do."

Mom looked from Kurt to Keri and back to Dad. "It's two more weeks of prevention in our own children." Her face was gray. There were dark circles under her eyes.

"Only one week," said Kurt. "There're four pills and four people. One, two, three, four." He pointed at each member of the family as he counted.

Mom shifted uncomfortably. How long had her parents only been pretending to take their medication while they saved it for her and Kurt?

Mom didn't look at Kurt. "I guess if we can trust God in two weeks, we can trust him now," she said.

Dad turned to the children. "What do you think?" he asked.

"I don't even like malaria pills!" Kurt said.

"I think we should share," Keri whispered. The pain in her stomach had settled into a dull ache. She remembered the high fever and racking chills when she had had the disease. She didn't want to go through that again, but she couldn't bear to think about what could happen to Sarita without the medication. If her parents could go without medication so that she and Kurt wouldn't get sick, she could go without it for Leila's little sister. "Give it to Sarita."

"Let's all go," Dad said.

Keri took her father's hand as they wound between the camouflaged shelters. It was the first time she had held his hand since they left Pastor Makusa behind. He started and then smiled and squeezed hers. There was nothing he could have done to save Pastor Makusa. Keri knew that now. He had only been trying to protect her and Kurt and Mom. But there was something they could all do to save Sarita. They would do it.

Mamani Argentina sat on a stool outside the commander's

137

shelter, rocking her child. Neither the warmth of the sun nor the woolen blanket she was wrapped in seemed to touch the little girl. Sarita trembled with chills. Her mother's dark eyes were puffy. Leila sent anxious looks from beside the cooking fire where she stirred a large pot.

Commander Dube was sitting at a table in the shade. He had a pile of papers in front of him, but he kept glancing toward *Mamani* Argentina. When the Andersons stopped in front of his hut, he rose.

"*Senhor comandante,*" Dad began. "We came to this country to share the love of Jesus Christ and the things that he has given us. We would like to ask God to use this medicine to heal Sarita."

He held out the bottle to the commander. Dube studied the label. He gave Dad a questioning look and spilled the tablets into his hand.

"This isn't a full treatment," he said. "Even for a child."

"I know," Dad replied. "But it's all we have left. Healing comes from God with or without medicine."

"And if one of you gets sick?" The commander's question hung in the air as he fingered the small plastic bottle in his hand.

"Healing comes from God with or without medication," Dad repeated in a steady voice. Keri thought he didn't look quite so pale.

Commander Dube's face gave away no emotion.

"Give it to her, woman," he said after a moment. He pressed the bottle into *Mamani* Argentina's hand. His eyes lingered on the child's face before he turned back to the table.

"Let's pray," Dad said. He knelt and laid both hands on Sarita's dark braids.

❧

When night fell, Dad returned with Kurt to their shelter. Mom sat with *Mamani* Argentina. Sometimes Mom read aloud from the Portuguese Bible, and sometimes they just sat silently.

"Let me stay, too," Keri begged. Leila stood very close to her and held her hand.

"All right," Mom agreed.

The girls prepared the supper and carried food to the men. Tomé stuffed it into his face. His father seemed distracted and ate little. Mfana hovered on the edge of the firelight and ate what he was given.

Leila carried a plate to the women sitting with Sarita, and Keri brought them sweet tea. Mom coaxed *Mamani* Argentina to drink a little although her part of the food on the plate they shared remained untouched. When the chills turned to fever, the girls carried cool water to bathe the child, but it didn't seem to do much good.

Keri sat by the fire while Leila scrubbed the pot with sand. The light flickered orange on Mfana's skin where he watched from a short distance. He never seemed to stop watching her or Kurt. Tonight she was glad for his quiet company.

At last Mfana disappeared to wherever it was he slept, and the girls fell asleep clinging to one another on a *capulana* spread by the fire.

It was early morning when Keri woke to the sound of a woman's wail. It echoed through her soul with all the grief and loss that had ever been. Leila woke and trembled. Keri put her arm around her friend, and they walked toward the door. Sarita was dead.

CHAPTER 14

"It's too hot," Keri said when lessons were done one afternoon. Temperatures had risen daily since Commander Dube took five men and stomped into the bush the day after the funeral. He said he was going to check on negotiations, but Keri was sure he couldn't stand to be in camp with all the memories of Sarita.

She flapped her T-shirt to create a breeze. It was almost as steamy as January in Maputo. "It's got to rain soon. Look at those clouds."

Thunderheads were forming in the east. They had built up yesterday and the day before. Each day they raised everyone's hopes of relief, but each day they passed over without leaving a drop of moisture.

Leila pulled a piece of grass and twiddled it in her fingers. She didn't even look at the sky.

"Let's go to the spring," Keri suggested. "You promised you'd show me how to make a farm." In America, she would have considered herself too old for make believe, but no one would laugh at her here, and Leila needed cheering up.

Keri got to her feet. "Come on. It'll be cooler there." Leila followed.

The girls splashed through the shallow water downstream from the water carriers. Cool drops splattered Keri's legs and the hem of her skirt. It wasn't the same without Sarita and her corncob doll. She glanced at Leila. She wished there were something she could say or do to make it right.

Kurt's shout came from a nearby slope. Keri looked up to see him hanging upside down from the branches of a cashew tree. Mfana searched the ground below him.

"How about there?" Keri suggested. She pointed to a spot where the stream curved around a large flat rock. Earth had drifted against it like the sloping sides of a mountain. It reached in two ridges to embrace a smooth space that sloped gently down to the water.

"All right." Leila nodded without interest.

"What do we do?" Keri plopped on her knees in the water.

They planned where the huts should go and stuck sticks in the ground in circles. Leila showed Keri how to weave strips of bark in and out to form the walls. Keri had envisioned something like sand castles on the beach. This was much more like building an African dollhouse, complete in every detail. The black clay from the bank of the stream felt cool under her fingers as she daubed it into the frames.

Leila gathered dry grass to thatch the *rondavels*. She tied bundles into sprays to spread on top and trimmed them neatly with her teeth.

"There. Now we can take the roof off to get inside," she explained. She seemed more alive than she had in days.

Keri surveyed their work. Sarita would have loved it. Leila's eyes were moist and distant. She must have been thinking the same thing.

"We could make a garden over here," Keri suggested. She began to dig an irrigation ditch from the stream and search for tiny shoots to plant in neat rows. It felt good to have her feet part way into the cool water. The air was thick with humidity and the thunderclouds heaped themselves like huge plates of fluffy porridge.

They had been working hard for more than an hour when Keri smelled smoke. She looked up to see the boys squatting in a sandy spot a few meters above them.

"What are you doing?" she asked. At home they weren't allowed to play with fire, but Africans seemed to take it for granted.

"Roasting cashews," Kurt replied. He pointed out a little heap of nuts. Some of them clung to bits of over-ripe fruit where they had been broken off from the base. They were still in their thick green outer casings.

Mfana blew gently on a neatly arranged pile of twigs and fed it more wood.

"You have to make sure they're well roasted," Kurt explained. "Because they're full of poison gas."

"I know." Once as a small child Keri had bitten one. She may as well have bitten a firecracker. The poison ran like acid over her lips and chin. Even though her mother washed her as fast as she could, it left an ugly red mark that stung for hours.

Mfana silently tended his coals. Leila squatted beside

them and shook the sand off the flat piece of tin the boys had brought. When the African children judged the coals ready, Mfana spread them with a stick, and Leila placed the tin over them. They scattered the cashews on top, and Leila shook the pan gently, gripping it with her bunched skirt when it grew hot.

"Get back," she ordered.

One of the husks exploded like a tiny bomb. Keri jerked away. Orange flames curled around the nut case. Two more exploded in quick succession with a sound like gunfire that made the sharp pain start up in Keri's stomach.

"You have to burn off all the gas," Mfana explained, "without burning the nuts inside."

He scooted back and quickly dug a hole, heaping sand between his legs. Every green husk was burning now and quickly turning black.

"Ready," said Leila. She tipped the pan into the hole, and Mfana pushed the heap of sand over the nuts to smother the flames.

The children knelt around the hole, looking at each other. Leila grinned in anticipation. Keri grinned back. After a few moments, Mfana scooped his hands into the sand and pushed it away to expose the buried treasure. Kurt grabbed greedily at a nut.

"Ouch!" he cried, dropping it. He plunged his burnt fingers into his mouth, and Mfana laughed at him.

Leila batted a few nuts around, letting them cool in the air before she picked one up. Mfana already had a fist-sized stone in his hand. He tapped lightly on the charred husk of a nut he placed on one of the flat boulders. Bits of black fell away, exposing the curled cashew inside. He popped it into his mouth and picked up another.

"Let me try!" Kurt grabbed a nut and smashed it between rocks. The nut crumbled into so many fragments it would be impossible to separate them from the burnt husk. His face fell.

Keri laughed. "Gently, silly," she teased.

She gingerly picked up a nut. It was warm between her fingers, but not hot. She laid it on a boulder and tapped it gently with another stone. By the time she got the black husk off, the nut was broken in several pieces, but it was warm and delicious.

"Now I know why cashews are so expensive," she said.

The children cracked and ate and cracked and ate.

"Is that all?" asked Kurt.

Mfana explored the hole thoroughly. "That's all."

Keri turned to Leila. "Let's go back to our farm."

"OK." Leila got to her feet. "I want to finish the thorn-bush fence."

"Are you making a farm?" asked Kurt. "We could make a road to it and then the rebels could attack."

"You'd better not attack our farm!" Keri turned on him angrily. "We put a lot of work into it."

"Let us see it anyway."

They clambered over the rocks to where the tiny huts nestled between the mountain and the curve of the river. The leaves in the garden waved gently in the slight breeze that had sprung up.

Keri straightened the thatch on one of the huts. "See!"

"What's that?" Kurt asked, pointing to a handful of white pebbles clustered behind one of the huts.

"Those are the goats," Leila replied.

Mfana stared at the little farm without saying anything. He squatted on his heels beside it.

"There should be another hut," he said abruptly.

"OK," said Keri. "Where?"

Mfana knelt down and brushed away a pile of seeds that Leila had arranged for the grain store. "The father's hut is here in the center," he announced.

He began to shape the frame with a door facing the stream.

"I'll make another roof," Leila offered. She trotted off to where she had gotten the dry grass.

"Hey, we were going to make a road," Kurt complained. "Remember? Let's make a road and attack the *coluna*."

Mfana didn't seem to hear him.

"The goats should be by the mountain," he said. He scooped up the handful of pebbles and scattered it where the sand formed the lower slope.

"Hey!" said Keri. "What are you doing?" A chilly breeze ruffled her hair, and she looked up to see the clouds turning dark. Perhaps the rains would come today.

Mfana ignored her protest. "Where's the boy to watch the goats?" he demanded.

"We didn't make any people yet," Keri admitted.

Mfana darted away and broke thick twigs from a shrub. "Three grown-ups and seven children," he announced when

146

he came back. "Here's the mother and the father." He placed two tall sticks outside the huts. "Here's the auntie." He had another tall stick in his hand. "Where's the fire? The auntie needs a fire to cook with."

"Here's the fire." Leila showed him where she had made a tiny circle of pebbles to mark the fireplace.

"No, no! Not there!" Mfana swept the pebbles away and arranged them behind the auntie's hut. He placed her carefully beside it.

Keri watched him. She wanted to say, "This is our game; go build your own farm," but her tongue was glued to the back of her teeth. Something told her this was more than a game.

"Here's the baby." He broke off a small twig and started to put it by the mother and father. "We have to tie it to her back. She has to have the baby on her back." He looked frantically for something that would serve.

"Here," said Keri. She tore a ragged strip from her skirt. "We could make her a *capulana*, too." She ripped a wider piece and handed both to Mfana. He fumbled with the knot. "Let me do it." Keri tied the *capulana* neatly around the mother and bound the baby to her back. Mfana watched her intently.

"There," Keri said. Mfana took the mother doll reverently in his hands.

"The big girl went away." Mfana tossed one stick over his shoulder. He put two children by the auntie and two more by the mother's hut.

"The big boy watches the goats." There was pride as well

as certainty in his voice as he placed his last stick in the middle of the white pebbles. He sat down with his ankles crossed and his arms draped lazily over his knees as Keri had seen herdboys sit.

"We need a pen for the goats." He jumped up again.

"I'll help." Kurt knelt by the farm. Mfana handed him some stiff grass like the straws in the broom at home and showed him how to break it off and stick pieces in the dirt.

"That looks exactly like a cane fence!" Keri said. She laughed and told herself it really was just a game. "You're good at making things, Mfana."

Soon a small corral stood between the vegetable gardens and the mountain. Mfana began to move the goats into it, one by one.

"Let me do it," begged Kurt.

"No." Mfana pushed him aside. "I'm the herdboy."

When all the goats were in the corral, he added more straws to close the fence. "Now they eat." He pulled a leaf from a bush and placed it on the ground near the auntie's hut, arranging the women and children on it.

"What about the Daddy?" asked Kurt.

"He already ate," Mfana informed him. "Now they sleep."

He lifted the lids of the huts and put the auntie and her children in one and the mother and father and the other children in another.

"There's no moon. The night is dark." His voice was quiet and took on the cadence of storytelling.

Keri looked up and saw her mother and *Mamani* Argentina watching them. Storm clouds blackened the sky, and

Keri was sure they had come to call the children back to camp, but they didn't.

"From around the side of the mountain come the bandits. They steal all the goats." With a sudden violent movement, Mfana crushed one side of the little fence and swept the goats out of the pen.

Kurt let out a startled cry. Leila drew back. Keri couldn't take her eyes off Mfana.

"Then the herdboy comes out." Mfana's voice was the whisper of someone who didn't want to disturb the sleepers. Thunder rumbled someplace over their heads, but Keri couldn't tear her eyes off the boy. He lifted the roof of the parent's hut and brought out the thick twig that had been on the hillside. He gripped it for a moment. The muscles of his neck stood out like tight cords. His body trembled. Slowly he stood up.

He darted toward the fire. Coals still glowed where the children had roasted cashews. He leapt back as fast as he had gone, waving a glowing stick in his hand. He plunged the stick into the thatch of one of the toy huts.

"And he burned the house down!" His voice trembled like the approaching thunder.

The thatch of the first house blazed up, and Mfana plunged the stick into the auntie's house.

"No, Mfana! No! The herdboy wouldn't do that!" Keri tried to wrestle the stick from his hand. Thunder crashed, loudly this time. The sky blazed with lightning. It was reflected in Kurt's frightened eyes as he crouched against a tree.

"His family's inside! He wouldn't! He wouldn't!" It couldn't happen that way because she didn't want it to happen that way.

"He had to! The bandits made him." Mfana struggled with the stick and thrust it into the third hut even as huge drops of rain exploded in the dust around them. "They said they'd kill him. They had knives and a gun. He had to! Don't you see?"

All the little huts were burning now. Keri wanted to brush the thatch away and rescue the pieces of wood trapped inside, but Mfana stomped on the garden and the corral and stepped on her hand. He brought his bare feet down on the huts, scattering the blazing grass and trampling the walls into oblivion.

"He had to kill them!" he screamed. "Don't you know? They made him do it! They made him!"

"He wouldn't, would he, Mama?" Keri looked desperately at her mother.

Tears were streaming down her mother's face as she slowly reached out a hand to Mfana. "Dzumisana?" she said.

Mfana froze. He turned his head slowly and looked at Mom. His eyes held all the terror of a young goat dragged to the slaughter. Bits of grass blazed under his bare toes, but the boy ignored them.

"Dzumisana," Mom said again, reaching out both her arms. "Let us give praise. You are found. Your grandfather Makusa loved you so much."

Mfana took a long slow breath. He kicked the straw away and leaped up the hillside as the rain began to fall.

CHAPTER 15

"Mfana!" Keri shouted as she ran after him.

"Keri!" She heard her mother call, but didn't stop. Mfana bounded ahead of her over rocks and through the sparse yellow grass that waved wildly in the gusting wind. He headed toward the scattered cashew trees. Their branches made a twisted pattern against the steely gray sky.

"Mfana!" she called. "Dzumisana!"

How could her mother have known his real name was Dzumisana? He had never told them any name but Mfana, "boy." Then she remembered Pastor Makusa's story—the farm between the odd flat mountain and the curve of the river, the son who had brought his brother's widow to live with them, the little girl, Rute, who had gone to Chibuto to help her grandmother and go to school.

It all fit. That was why they hadn't found the body of the oldest boy. The rebels had . . . Keri couldn't bear to think of what the rebels had forced him to do, to put the guilt of murder on the soul of a child and turn a herdboy, loved by his grandfather, into a killer.

The rain poked her back with all the force of taunting

fingers. "Nothing is fair," it seemed to say. "God doesn't care." Her wet denim skirt, ragged after weeks of wear, chafed her legs. Her hair hung in wet hanks, which channeled cold water down her face and neck.

Dzumisana's legs were longer, and he had more practice running barefoot in the bush. The gap widened between them. Thunder crashed again when Keri reached the cashew grove, and her eyes searched the tangled branches. He wasn't there. By the time she reached the open again, his course was hidden by a curtain of heavy rain.

"Mfana!" she called as she stumbled on. Her voice seemed to bounce back at her from the wall of falling water. "Dzumisana! Come home!" There was no answer but a flash of lightning and a deafening clap of thunder that made her jump convulsively.

Keri paused to catch her breath. She was trembling with cold after the heat of the day.

Come home, she had said. Dzumisana had no home. The farm between the mountain and the river was burned and overrun like the miniature one by the stream. His family was gone. His grandfather had been left behind by the rebels. Keri was sure he was dead by now, although Kurt continued to pray for *Vovô Pastor* every night.

Keri remembered Pastor Makusa's wife, *Mamani* Jordina, sitting under the mango tree in Chibuto, breaking corn from the cob or embroidering a tablecloth with colored threads picked from worn-out pieces of fabric. She saw the face of Rute, smiling under her water tin. There would be a home for Dzumisana. Keri was sure of that.

She stumbled on, searching for signs of the way he might have gone. Her breath came ragged, and her side cramped.

"Ouch!" She pulled a long thorn from her right foot and limped forward. There was a bloody gash on her left big toe. She hoped she wouldn't meet a wild animal. It was hopeless to think of finding Dzumisana in the wilderness. She had been foolish to try. Maybe she should turn back.

She looked behind her. She had no idea how far she had come. She wasn't even certain of the way. She could no longer see the grove of cashew trees or the stream. All that was visible were thorn bushes and acacia trees and tall grass beaten down by the rain. She was lost.

Blue showed in the east. The thunderhead could be clearly distinguished to the north, trailing a wet curtain of gray over the countryside below.

An abandoned anthill rose higher than Keri's head. She dropped down beside it and rinsed her toe in a shallow puddle.

She leaned back against the hard plastered sides of the anthill and closed her eyes. Her thoughts swirled like the last water around the drain in the washtub at home. All emotion seemed to have been sucked down a dark hole. She fell asleep.

"*Que é isso?*" The voice of Commander Dube was sharp. He stood over her with his hands on his hips. Keri blinked and was relieved to see that he wasn't carrying a weapon. She tried to scramble to her feet, but he grabbed her arm and dragged her after him. The five men who had accompanied him stood in a path marked with long ruts still filled with water.

"You aren't going to run away now that we've arranged this business!" Tomé leered at her from behind his father's back. Keri wondered what kind of business had been arranged.

"Ow!" she cried. The commander loosened the clamp of his fingers on her arm, but not enough to allow her to get away.

"*Vamos.*" He dragged her through the bush.

༄

The sun was setting as they reentered the camp. Its brilliant orange rays glittered from millions of raindrops. The world looked clean and new.

Dube threw Keri to the ground in the center of camp. "I found this alone in the bush!" He made it sound like she was no more than a piece of baggage left behind. Keri shivered in the cold mud. "Who is responsible?"

"Everyone is looking for her!" Pedro explained meekly.

"Thank God you're found!" breathed Mom. She knelt in the mud and clutched Keri to her.

"Where's the man?" Dube demanded.

"He is searching. Mangani and Zé are with him."

"Find them!"

"The boy is gone, too—Mfana."

Dube made a dismissive gesture. "He'll be back. He has nowhere to go."

"Did you find him?" Kurt whispered. His eyes were wide and dark.

Keri shook her head. Mom brought a cloth and a bowl of water and washed the mud from her face. She carefully bathed the cut on her toe and cleaned the scratches of thorns.

"You're all right?" Dad's face was grim when he arrived back.

Commander Dube strode up to them. "Tonight we start for the border," he announced. They all looked at him in surprise. "The government has agreed to our demands. You will be delivered to officials of the Red Cross in Zimbabwe in three days. Prepare to march."

Although Commander Dube was anxious to be on the way, it took several hours for the party to be organized. He would escort them to the border. From there, they would be taken to Mutare in Zimbabwe. The American ambassador and several congressmen would meet them. At last the resistance would get the recognition it deserved as a force in the region.

"You might have been released a month ago if the big men could have fit it into their schedules," Dube sneered.

When he was gone, Mom gathered their few possessions and slipped them into the backpack.

She brushed a strand of straggling hair behind her ear with a thin hand. "I will miss *Mamani* Argentina very much," she mused. "In all the years we've lived in Africa, for the first time, I had nothing to give but myself." Her voice trembled, and the muscles of her face twitched. "With Argentina . . . that was enough."

Keri could hardly hear the last words as they were swallowed in tears. Dad wrapped his arms around Mom and patted her shoulder like a small child.

Keri blinked back tears she didn't understand. She pulled her holey socks over feet tender from her wild run through the bush. The rubber soles of her shoes were cracked and the laces nearly worn through. *I ought to be happy we're going home.* But she wasn't any happier than her mother. Her heart was a heavy lump in her chest. How could they leave Dzumisana behind?

"*Com liçensa.*" *Mamani* Argentina knelt at the low opening to the shelter. Mom tearfully embraced her friend. *Mamani* Argentina held out a packet wrapped in banana leaves.

"Provisions for the journey," she whispered. The packet smelled of roasted chicken with wild garlic.

"You must take care of Mfana," Mom explained as she wiped away her tears. "Make him wash and eat right. He's only a hurt little boy even if he tries to act like an evil man."

The African woman nodded.

"His name is Dzumisana," Mom said. "Call him Dzumisana. Let him know he's a person with a family and a hope."

Leila took Keri's hand. "I'll never forget you, Keri," she whispered shyly. Keri threw her arms around her young friend's neck.

"I won't forget you either, Leila."

"My real papa's name is Fernando Campos in Nauela," the girl explained. "You'll tell him I love him, won't you?"

"I'll try," said Keri. Maybe her father would know how to

get a message to Lomweland. "Someday you'll get home and go to school. I know you will. I'll ask my dad if we can leave you the Bible. That way you can practice reading it to your mother."

Leila's smile brightened.

"Leila." Now it was Kurt who acted shy. His fingers slid nervously back and forth over the small object in his hand. "Would you give this to Mfana, I mean, Dzumisana, please. His grandfather made it for him." He held out the hardly recognizable ox.

"He made it for you, Kurt," Keri said. She could feel the pain in her stomach beginning.

Kurt shook his head. "He made it for me because I reminded him of his grandson. Dzumisana should have it to remind him of his grandfather. It's an ox," he explained when Leila looked doubtful. "See, that's where the legs and horns used to be."

Leila took it in her hand and carefully turned it over.

"Dzumisana will understand," Kurt said.

❧

It was only because everyone was so busy with preparations for the journey that Keri was able to evade Pedro's watchful eye and slip away to the stream. It was quiet there. Moonlight glittered from the silver thread of water tracing its way down the hill toward *Mamani* Argentina's village.

Keri picked her way over stones and puddles to the sight of their imaginary farm. The play garden she had carefully

157

planted in the afternoon lay trampled in the mud. The charred roofs of the tiny huts had been scattered to the wind. Their walls were crushed and beaten by the rain and trampled by frantic feet.

She had been angry earlier. She had begged and pleaded with her father not to leave until they could take Dzumisana with them. Her father's eyes had been full of anguish, but Commander Dube had insisted they would never take Dzumisana with them.

"He is one of us," he swore. "His family would never want him back after all he has done. The government would hang him for murder." The tenderness he had shown for Sarita was nowhere to be seen. Keri was pretty sure the government wouldn't hang a child who was forced to murder, but she wouldn't put it past Dube to hang him for running away.

"Dad, please! They have to let him come!" Keri insisted.

"Keri, we don't even know where he is. We can't wait. Much as I might like to, we have to think of Kurt and your mother. She needs a doctor. She needs a doctor soon. It has taken two months to arrange this meeting with the Red Cross. We have to be there."

Keri could see in his eyes that he wanted to take Dzumisana as much as she did, but he couldn't imagine Commander Dube changing his mind. Dube saw nothing but the soldier. He couldn't see the child that was locked inside.

Keri looked at her mother resting on a mat. Her cheeks were sunken, and her skin was yellow. Dad was right. They had to go.

Keri smelled the acrid stench of wet ash as she passed

the little fire they had used to roast cashews. It seemed an eternity ago.

The water, rocks, and low shrubs all showed different shades of gray against the starry sky. Keri knelt by the remains of the farm and felt around in the mud for the sticks that had inhabited it. It seemed as if to hold them would allow her to mourn the real family that had perished. There was nothing there. Her shoulders shook with sobs.

"Dzumisana, where are you?" she cried.

A shadow moved. Two large white eyes looked at her.

"Dzumisana?"

He turned slowly away, clutching something in his hands. He knelt on the ground with his back to her. Keri knelt beside him. In the earth in front of him were eight small holes in a row. From his hand, the boy took a stick and laid it in the first grave. The denim *capulana* around it was badly charred, but a smaller bit of wood was still lashed to it. Dzumisana laid another charred stick at the other end of the row and one in the middle. He arranged the children in between. Every movement was slow and deliberate and full of dignity. Keri bit her lip so hard it hurt. She helped Dzumisana mound dirt over the miniature graves.

When they had finished, he picked up the small white hawthorn blossoms at his side and pressed their stems carefully into the loose dirt. His eyes were puffy, and his cheeks hung slack and hopeless. Keri wondered where he had been since the storm. Tears ran down her cheeks. When she looked at Dzumisana, his head was bowed and his eyes were closed.

"Jesus, help us," Keri prayed silently. "Make him know that you love him."

Dzumisana glanced behind him.

"Keri!" She heard Dad's call from the edge of the camp. It must be time to go. The weight of sorrow seemed to crush Dzumisana's thin shoulders. She reached out a hand to touch his arm. He stared at it for a long moment.

"We're going to Zimbabwe," Keri whispered. "Come with us!"

His eyes bored into her as though wanting to rip away all pretense and know if she really meant it. "Rute is in Chibuto. And *Mamani* Jordina, your grandmother. You have a family. They want you; I know they do."

"Keri!" Dad's voice was nearer.

"Commander Dube says you can't come, but he won't know if you follow. You know the way to Zimbabwe. You've been there before, you said."

He nodded slowly, but Keri wasn't sure if he meant that he knew the way or that he would come.

"Only, be careful," she warned. "Commander Dube mustn't know."

He made no sign that he heard. He was still kneeling with his head bowed when she slipped away.

"Coming, Dad!"

CHAPTER 16

They started well before dawn and walked all that day. It was no longer necessary to move at night since the agreement for their release. Commander Dube still hustled them under the scanty cover of an acacia when a single engine plane passed, but he didn't seem very concerned.

Only four soldiers accompanied them besides Commander Dube. Pedro and Tomé carried Mom between them on a litter. Kurt, Keri, and Dad helped carry sleeping rolls and cooking supplies. If Keri hadn't been so worried about her mother, it might have seemed more like a camping trip than a military mission.

It had been over two months since the Andersons were captured, and in a few days they would be home. Keri was completely free of stomachaches for the first time in weeks. She was actually happy except for the moments when she remembered Dzumisana. "God, make him follow us," she prayed as she trotted after Tomé. "Don't let him stay with the rebels."

There was a thundershower in the afternoon. Commander

Dube never slackened the pace. It was a good thing the rebels and the government had come to an agreement. In a few weeks mud would make the trails impassable. In the evening they feasted on the roast chicken *Mamani* Argentina had given them. It was probably because of the heat, but Mom didn't even suggest that they save some for the next day.

When Keri woke in the morning there was a small ripe mango by her head. She sniffed the flowery scent. It must have come from *Mamani* Argentina's basket. Mom knew it was Keri's favorite.

She rolled over to smile her thanks, but her mother was still sleeping. Her head was pillowed on her arm. The top of it nestled into Dad's chest.

Keri raised herself on her elbow. Everyone was still sleeping—even the guard. Commander Dube never would have allowed such laxness before.

Keri slit the skin of the mango with her fingernail and peeled it back. She sunk her teeth into the juicy flesh. Then she remembered. There had been no mangos in *Mamani* Argentina's gift. It was still too early in the season, and ripe ones were hard to find.

She let her eyes search the bush around them. There was no sound or movement.

"Dzumisana?" she whispered.

The guard snorted and shifted his position. There was no other response.

❧

The bush grew thicker as they moved west. Walking became easier when they came upon the overgrown remnants of a road. Keri walked beside the litter. Dad walked on the other side holding Kurt's hand. Sometimes Mom walked for a while to give Tomé and Pedro a break, but she couldn't keep it up for long.

"I'm sorry I'm so weak." She grimaced from the cramps in her stomach.

The ground climbed slowly, and they saw the Chimanimani Mountains in the distance.

"Zimbabwe!" Dad pointed to the line of cool green hills.

"Is that where we're going?" Kurt asked. He had been restless in the night, but if he cried out with a nightmare, Keri was too deeply asleep to hear. He didn't stink of urine this morning either.

"I think so," Dad replied.

As they drew near, the mountains rose ahead of them. Ridge upon ridge of deep blue shaded into murky gray until it blended into the humid sky. In the late afternoon dark clouds formed over the highest peaks. Keri could distinguish the distant line where rain began and ended. She longed for its coolness to fall on her.

The party broke off from the road and descended a thickly wooded bank. Keri heard the sound of rushing water over the tramping of feet and voices of men.

"Look!" cried Kurt. A river fifty feet across stretched ahead of them, but Kurt wasn't pointing to the river. High above it rose the concrete arches of a bridge.

Dad stared, hands on hips. "This must have been one of

the main routes linking Mozambique with the farms of Eastern Zimbabwe," he said. "What a waste." He shook his head slowly and turned away.

The high span of the bridge was broken. Chunks of cement hung by rusted cables of steel above the water. Giant blocks lay where they had fallen in the riverbed.

"Bombed in the Rhodesian War," Dube informed them. He swatted a mosquito.

"We must be very near the border," Dad said.

"Another day, if you can keep up the pace." Commander Dube sent Tomé to fetch the ferryman from a hut under the broken arch.

"Of course we can keep up the pace," Keri said, but she didn't say it out loud. It was all she could do not to search the bush behind them for signs that Dzumisana might be following. The last thing she wanted was to alert the commander.

By the time the kettle was boiled and tea made, a badly weathered dugout canoe pulled up on the bank. It was nothing more than a hollowed-out tree without the hint of a keel to stabilize it. A thin black man with skin as wrinkled as hippo leather stood beside it, holding a long pole.

Commander Dube nodded for Tomé to direct the packing of bundles into the bottom of the boat.

Mom gave Keri a small orange from their provisions as a gift for the ferryman. She handed it to him respectfully with two hands. He didn't seem to know any Portuguese, but he smiled broadly, showing bare purple gums. He bobbed his thanks and clapped his hands together in the African way.

"It's time to cross," Commander Dube announced. "You first." He herded Mom and Kurt toward the round-bottomed boat.

It took two men to hold the craft steady while Pedro climbed in. The commander motioned Kurt forward, and Mom followed. She waved cheerily at Keri on the bank, but her face was tense.

When everything was steady, the ferryman pushed off and stepped into the stern. He levered his pole gently against the muddy river bottom. At first the river was shallow, but soon they passed into a more rapidly moving current. The ferryman had to push his pole deeper to reach the bottom. The boat wobbled as it drifted downstream.

Keri searched the banks for signs of crocodiles. She knew they liked to pull you under and drown you. They came back to eat you later. They could easily upset a fragile canoe like this one. She saw nothing but logs and dead branches lying in the water.

The dugout bumped the opposite bank. Pedro leaped on shore and held it steady while the others climbed out. As the ferryman returned, Mom and Kurt waved from the opposite bank with more confidence than they had shown before.

The dugout had already reached them when Keri remembered she had intended to check her shoelace when they made a stop. Only a few threads held it together. She knelt down and started to unlace the shoe and make a knot.

"*Vamos! Vamos!* We have to be in Zimbabwe tomorrow, you know!" Commander Dube sounded impatient. Tomé had already entered the bow and arranged the bundles.

Oh, well, Keri thought, *I can fix it on the other side of the river while they do the last trip*. She clambered into the dugout. It wobbled sickeningly under her, and she slowed her movements.

"Easy," Dad warned. The craft swayed. The ferryman stepped in and gently pushed off from the shore.

Keri breathed slowly as though even the movement of air in and out of her lungs could send them off balance. She barely moved her head as she looked first upstream and then down. There was movement in the brush at the top of the bank they had just left. It couldn't be a crocodile, not that far above the water. Perhaps one of the rebels was scouting for a safer place to cross. The canoe angled slightly downstream, and she could see the two remaining rebels still waiting nervously with the commander.

"Keri, hold still!" her father commanded as the canoe wobbled dangerously in the current.

They were opposite a pile of fallen masonry. The disruption in the flow had built an underwater sandbar midstream. Water plants waved soggy tentacles toward them. The front of the dugout passed the shallow spot and entered the faster current. Keri felt a slight pull.

The bow jerked to the right. Keri gripped the sides to keep her balance and tried desperately not to overcompensate. She could see Tomé's nails turning pale pink under the pressure of his grip.

Water dripped from the pole raised beside her. Slimy green leaves came with it from the bottom. The pole man shook it gently. That might have worked if he had been the only one in his homemade canoe, but just at that moment Tomé turned around. His eyes were wide and his face tense.

The canoe teetered once. Twice! Everyone in it swung in different directions, trying to restore the balance. The ferryman tumbled free. The push from his flying feet sent the unbalanced craft rotating rapidly in the opposite direction. Keri plunged into the stream.

The muffled sounds of thrashing bodies reached her over the low throb of the river flowing in her ears. A deep channel rushed past the sandbar. Her shoes filled quickly and pulled her down. Holding her breath, Keri opened her eyes and saw her father's black boots kicking toward the sunlight above her. The current dragged her away from him. Her feet touched the muddy bottom, and she pushed off with all her strength. The shoe on her left foot loosened.

The lace! It must have broken. She curled her toes in a desperate effort to hang on. In a moment her head broke the surface. She gasped for air.

She was far downstream, and the current was carrying her farther. The water frothed furiously where Commander Dube and the other rebels had jumped in. They appeared to be attempting to rescue her father who was an excellent swimmer. He already stood on the sand bank, scanning the surface. He had hold of a wet and trembling Tomé. Keri waved.

Dad motioned toward the far shore. He urged Tomé ahead of him and swam with him in a rescue grip. Mom beckoned from the bank. Keri kicked powerfully toward her.

It was then that she lost her shoe.

"No!" she cried, grabbing for it too late. She dove back into the cloudy depths, searching. How could she walk to Zimbabwe with one shoe? Mud and half decayed water plants floated around her, but she could see no broken-laced canvas shoe. She thrust her head above the water and drew air hungrily into her lungs.

The river curved to the northwest. Beyond where any of the watchers on the bank could see, something thrashed in the water.

One of the rescuers, she thought. "Hey! Catch my shoe!" she called.

"Keri!" She heard her mother's frantic scream above the splash of her own strokes. She stopped to dog paddle. Her father had reached the bank and crashed through the brush toward her. Everyone else pointed to where a brown log slid into the far side of the river.

Then she realized that logs don't slide into rivers by themselves. Crocodiles do.

CHAPTER 17

Keri forgot the lost shoe and the other swimmer and struck out for the bank as hard as she could. Her arms pulled at the water and thrust her body toward the shore.

Wet leaves brushed her legs, and she willed herself not to think that they could be anything other than plants. She was still swimming when her knee brushed the mud and her hand clawed the bank. She scrambled to her feet and dashed for the bush. As swift as a crocodile is in the water, he is slow and awkward on land, and the farther she got from the river, the safer she would be.

Dad clasped her tightly almost before she saw him. "You're safe," he whispered as she collapsed in his arms. His grip was fierce.

She looked up when the others joined them. Kurt grabbed her hand and squeezed it until the bones popped. Mom hugged her long and hard. Her body trembled against Keri like birch leaves in a breeze. They both breathed in ragged gasps.

The crocodile seemed to have lost interest. He floated

downstream toward where Keri had seen the other swimmer. But she must have been mistaken. Everyone was here, and they had all come from upstream. It might have been another crocodile. . . .

"I lost my shoe," she said.

"At least you're all right," Mom whispered.

A search of the shoreline downstream did not reveal a worn-out canvas shoe with a broken lace. Commander Dube made two of the soldiers wade cautiously into the water to look while everyone else kept a close eye out for crocodiles. They found the bundle of cooking utensils, but most of the supplies were gone. So was the canoe.

The wrinkled little ferryman argued vehemently with the commander. He waved his arms, and a rapid stream of words spilled from his mouth.

"What's wrong?" Dad asked Pedro.

"He wants us to replace his boat."

"Replace his boat? How?"

Pedro shrugged. "It's probably snared downstream," he explained. "I expect Commander Dube will leave someone to help him search." He untied a bundle of cooking supplies and emptied river water from the kettle.

"You and you." Dube pointed out two of his men. "Help search for the boat. If you don't find it in a couple days . . ." He made an impatient gesture. "Help him make a new one. You can meet us back at camp." The ferryman looked satisfied.

Pedro grinned. "He's probably hoping for a new boat out of this." He shook water from one of the sleeping mats and rolled it back up. "We need his good will to get our supplies across the river."

"We'll camp up there," Commander Dube said when it was dark. He pointed to where the road continued along the top of the embankment.

Keri was relieved. She had assumed he would make them walk a few more hours to make up for lost time. *How will I ever get to Zimbabwe with only one shoe?* Her feet were tough, but not enough for the rocks and thorns of a long march. Pedro scrambled up the bank ahead of her. The thick calluses on his feet were cracked like an old shoe.

The track this side of the bombed bridge was even more overgrown than where they had come from. It had been a long time since anything but foot traffic had passed this way. The bush grew close and thick around them. Wild animals could lurk only a few meters away and never be seen. She knew there were panthers in the mountains. Commander Dube must have been thinking the same thing. He directed them to make camp in the most open spot near where the broken bridge dropped off to the river below. He even let them build a fire.

Keri sat on the edge of the circle of light as far from the heat as possible while the little band shared the last of the fruit from *Mamani* Argentina's basket and a little jerked impala. It was all they had to eat. Everything else had gone to the bottom of the river.

Keri wiped the sweat off her forehead and wondered how Commander Dube could stand to sit so close to the fire.

❧

It was still dark when Keri woke. She rolled over on the *capulana* beside her mother, and her hand touched something cold and damp.

Ugh. She pulled back. What could it be? She reached out slowly until her fingers touched wet canvas. She felt along its surface, encountering smooth rubber and a straggling lace.

My shoe! She looked around the dark clearing. The stars were fading, and the sky showed pale gray behind the black trees, but she could make out nothing that would tell her how the shoe had gotten there. She shook it out, in case something had crawled into it in the night, and slipped it on her foot. Even in the dark she could feel slits and tears. Something with sharp teeth had chewed it. There was hardly enough lace left to bind two sets of holes, but it stayed on her foot.

A shiver of joy mixed with fear went up Keri's spine. It had to be Dzumisana. What if Commander Dube suspected? Keri knew he wouldn't be gentle if he caught the boy.

She slipped quietly from her mat and made her way to the river. The water lapped gently on the muddy bank. The darkness was fading to a pearl gray light. Keri peered upstream and down, keeping a safe distance from any suspicious-looking logs. There was no sign of the boy they had called Mfana.

"God, help him to get to Zimbabwe."

Voices sounded from the top of the bank. The others must be awake. She climbed back to the camp. Commander Dube sat wrapped in a blanket. He looked awful.

"Malaria," her father whispered.

The commander threw off the blanket and stood stiffly. He gave instructions to the two men who would be staying behind, while Tomé rolled the blanket into a bundle.

"Today we meet the Red Cross," he said to Dad. His smile was too weak to convey confidence.

"Where will that be?" Dad asked. "Surely you can tell us now."

Dube hesitated. "The Red Cross is waiting in the town of Mutare just across the border into Zimbabwe. A plane will meet us on this side and take you the rest of the way."

"A plane?" Keri croaked. How could Dzumisana follow them in a plane? "Is it too far to walk?" Both parents looked at her as though she were out of her mind.

Commander Dube laughed. "Mutare is less than ten miles on the other side of that mountain. There's a path we take all the time; where do you think we buy our supplies? But I wasn't going to tell the government about it!" He tied his bedroll firmly. "No, we'll let them come to us on an abandoned farm well away from our usual route."

"Your shoe!" Mom said. Everyone stared at Keri's feet.

Keri looked nervously at Commander Dube. "I went for a walk by the river," she said. "Look. Something has chewed it and most of the lace is gone." She bent to examine the damage and to hide her red face. She hadn't told any lies. What she said was absolutely true.

"Thank God," Mom sighed while Dad bent to examine the shoe. "I didn't know how we would . . . " Her voice choked, and she lay back on the litter.

❧

They climbed steadily for two hours. Commander Dube breathed heavily, and the litter was awkward on the steep slopes. The land was different here. Green grass spread like mold in the shade of silver-trunked gum trees. Above them, clinging vines draped the lush forest of the mountainside. Everywhere Keri felt the clammy dampness that wafted from the distant sea to be trapped in the crevices of the hills.

She wondered where Dzumisana was. The road was easy to follow. Where was the secret path over the mountains?

It was at the third rest stop that Keri realized the commander was shaking. Tomé took a blanket from the roll he carried and wrapped it around him.

"Is he going to die?" asked Kurt. Keri remembered Sarita's limp little body first shaking with cold then burning with fever. "There's no more medicine," Kurt insisted when Dad didn't answer right away.

"I don't think he'll die, Kurt," Dad replied quietly. "He's a grown man, much stronger than Sarita. Perhaps he can get some medicine when we reach the Red Cross."

That seemed to satisfy the little boy, but he leaned close to his father and his large brown eyes remained fixed on the shivering commander.

It was a long rest. Commander Dube pushed aside the

blanket and rose with obvious effort. He checked the position of the sun.

"Move out!" he commanded without acknowledging his weakness.

The sun was just past midday when they were stopped by a washout. The recent rains had cut a ravine thirty feet straight down and at least fifty feet across. It stretched out of sight in both directions.

Dad looked at the sky. The afternoon thunderclouds were building. "This was made by yesterday's rain." He shook his head slowly. "I wouldn't want to be down there when it starts up again."

Dube shivered. "We'll go around it. Tomé, find a way."

Tomé plunged into the forest beside a huge boulder anchored to the ground by the roots of a giant fig tree. All of them scrambled to follow. Mom walked, and Pedro carried the litter.

By the time they reached the road again, Commander Dube was flushed with fever. He leaned on Tomé.

"Perhaps we should rest a while," Dad suggested.

"We can't rest; we must get to the farm or they will say I have tricked them. Negotiations won't be so easy the next time." Commander Dube placed one foot in front of the other. He looked as though he were about to fall over. Eventually he did.

Tomé leaped to catch him. He settled his father gently on the ground.

"You must leave me," Dube said.

"You need a doctor," Mom insisted. "You need medication."

"Tomé can bring some back to me. Pedro will stay."

Tomé protested.

"You will go," Dube insisted.

"I don't know where this farm is," the young man admitted.

"Neither does Pedro! Follow this road into the valley. The farm will be on your right. You'll know it by the row of gum trees that line the drive. The airstrip is on a ridge behind the house."

They made Dube as comfortable as they could with a bedroll and a bottle of water. Mom dampened a cloth and spread it over his eyes.

"You must keep it wet," she explained. Pedro nodded.

"Good-bye," said Keri. She put out her hand and Pedro shook it gravely. She wondered if she would ever again see this thin man with his slit earlobes and his ready smile.

"Hurry," the commander said. "If you aren't there an hour before sunset, they'll leave without you."

"An hour before sunset?" Dad asked.

"Mutare airfield has no lights. No one is allowed to land after the sun goes down. You must be at the farm in time to get there before sunset. This is your last chance."

"We'll make it," Dad said grimly.

CHAPTER 18

We're going home, Keri reminded herself with each step. She ought to be happy, but she wasn't. Where was Dzumisana? She hadn't seen any sign of him since finding her shoe that morning.

"It's not fair," she said to no one in particular. "It's not fair, God!" she repeated, knowing exactly to whom she wanted to say it. "You answered Mom and Dad's prayers to go home. But what about Sarita? What about Leila and Dzumisana and even Commander Dube? What about them?" She stomped along expecting some kind of answer or, at least, a thunderbolt from heaven to strike her dead for asking.

"You didn't protect Pastor Makusa!" That wasn't exactly true. The Spirit the rebels still whispered about had to have been God. That morning she had seen Kurt fumbling in the pocket where he used to keep the ox. His eyes were closed, and he moved his lips. She had no doubt that her little brother still prayed every single day for *Vovô Pastor*. Keri had stopped pretending weeks ago.

Didn't God care as much about Leila and *Mamani* Argentina as he did the Andersons? Why didn't he let *them* go home? *Mamani* Argentina had two little boys in the village. Keri wasn't sure how she would feel about being "rescued" and separated from them forever. They probably needed her more than Leila's older brothers and sisters in Lomweland. It was so complicated.

Her head was light with hunger, and there was a throbbing behind her eyes. She stubbed her toe on a rock. It bruised her foot through the torn rubber of the damaged shoe, and she limped a few steps. All the fears and worries she had known in the last two months seemed to press down on her.

"What about Dzumisana?" she demanded silently. "How could you let such awful things happen to him? How could you leave him to grow up to be a bandit and a murderer like Tomé?" She glared at the strong shoulders of the teenager carrying the front end of her mother's litter.

She didn't speak out loud, but the bitter words formed in her head and some of them slipped out through clenched teeth. She could feel the hot tears behind her eyes ready to boil over in despair. To reject God would leave a cavern of emptiness. But a God who played favorites wasn't the kind of God she wanted.

"Either you aren't strong enough or you don't care enough," she muttered. "If you aren't strong enough, then you aren't really God. If you don't care enough, then I don't want you!"

Pain fused into one lump that filled her stomach and

clenched her ribs like the roots of the fig tree around the boulder. "I'll just go back to America and stop caring, too!" She wasn't sure how she would convince her parents to leave Africa, but she knew she would.

She concentrated on Tomé's moving feet in front of her. "If Dzumisana is there when we get to Mutare, then I'll know that you're big enough and care enough."

Keri felt terribly wicked talking to God this way. But how else could she know? The whole family thought their ordeal was almost over. Keri knew her struggle had only begun. She was terrified at what it would mean.

"If you're really God, you can do it," she explained. "If you love him as much as you love me, you won't leave him with the rebels."

Maybe she should give God more time. Demanding that Dzumisana be there when they arrived in Mutare was a lot to ask. No. She knew if she didn't set a deadline, she would go on like Kurt. She refused to go through the motions of praying for something that would never happen and pretending she believed it would.

"This isn't a silly thing like asking Santa for a new stereo," Keri insisted. "This is about a real person just like me. I can't pretend. I have to know, and I have to know today."

The towering gums gave way to smaller trees. The hills were a little less steep and the rocky outcroppings less frequent. The forest grew sparse, and the trees looked young as though this had once been a pasture.

A stone wall ran along the side of the road. It had crumbled under the roots of a wild fig here or the weight of untrimmed bougainvillea there. Two stone posts rose ahead to mark the entrance to the former farm.

"There are the gum trees." Keri pointed. Two silver green lines of trees ran gracefully from the gate, down a slope, and up the hill on the far side.

Kurt ran excitedly ahead. The men put down the litter and stretched upright. Dad scanned the sky as though searching for a plane. The sun had long since dropped behind the mountain to the west and left them in shadow. Keri studied the golden light on the clouds. Sunset couldn't be far away.

"Dube said the avenue of gum trees would lead us to the house," Dad reminded them. "The airstrip's on the ridge beyond it."

"The house must be there," said Keri. She pointed to a grove on the next hill.

"I just hope we aren't too late," Dad said. "Come on, Tomé." They picked up the litter and started down the drive.

The sky was hidden from the shelter of the weed-choked avenue. They couldn't see the sun to know how near it was to setting. Nor was there a sign of an approaching or departing plane.

"Won't they wait for us?" Kurt asked.

"They won't want to spend the night here," Dad explained. The words came in short spurts. All his energy went into walking with the litter. "If they're late leaving, they won't be able to land in Mutare. No, they won't wait."

"Let's hurry." Kurt began to jog.

If God abandons us here, it will be my fault, Keri thought.

It's only what I deserve for talking to him that way. She ran ahead of Kurt.

The lane emerged in front of a square house surrounded by wide porches. A tangle of red and purple bougainvillea and orange honeysuckle covered the roof, which had collapsed under its weight. The windows and doors had been stripped from their holes, but otherwise it seemed unmolested. The farm had closed down before the war had reached it.

"What's that?" Keri said aloud. The sound of engines came from somewhere beyond the building. "The plane is leaving!"

She sprinted around the house. The drive was overgrown, but it still clearly indicated the way to the top of the ridge. The avenue of gums had ended. Bits of blue could be seen between the leaves of the lower trees like pieces of a jigsaw puzzle scattered on a green tabletop. Keri knew the pilot would never spot her beneath them.

To her left, a steep slope of large rocks reached out of the shadows and into the remaining sunlight. Keri plunged through a thicket of raspberries to reach it. They tore at her T-shirt and her bare arms. She had to stop that plane.

Her foot slipped on the first rock. She scraped her knee, and her palms were embedded with gravel. She brushed them off. She could feel her damaged shoe flapping loosely.

She came out at the top not fifty yards from a small Cessna at the end of the short runway. It turned away from her, prepared to take off.

"Stop!" screamed Keri, running toward it. "Stop!" She

waved her arms wildly over her head. She thrashed through the weeds and brush, which scratched her legs and plucked at her skirt.

"God help me!" she sobbed. "Please, help! It's all my fault!"

The plane gained speed and took off into the east. The sound grew quieter as it rose slowly and banked to the left.

CHAPTER 19

"God, help me!" Keri cried again, slowing her feet and dropping her arms. Sobs shook her body. "I'm sorry."

The sound of the engines increased. Keri looked through her tears. The plane was coming back! It made a wide sweep and headed across the farm as it gained height to clear the mountain. She began to wave her arms again.

She heard shouts from her right where the road left the trees. Kurt had reached the open field. He jumped up and down and waved. Dad and Tomé set down the litter and ran toward the strip.

The plane headed straight toward them. Keri ran into the cleared space of the landing strip. Surely the pilot would see her!

The Cessna was nearly above her when it's wing dipped twice, and it began to bank once more. It was coming back.

Even as she collapsed on the stubble of the field, she could hear the others cheering. The pilot circled the field once, positioning himself for the landing. He turned and taxied back to where the family had gathered on the end of the runway.

"You must be the Andersons," he shouted over the engines. He pushed his headset off thick curly brown hair. "Get in, quickly. We may still be able to convince Mutare to let us land."

"Wait!" insisted Mom. She leaned against the side of the plane. Her face was pale and exhausted. "Do you have any malaria medicine?" Dad hurried Kurt aboard.

"Malaria medicine?" The pilot hesitated only a moment. He reached beneath his seat. "I always keep some in my first aid kit." Mom snatched the bottle from him almost before he had it out of the plastic box. She pressed it into Tomé's hand.

"For the love of Jesus," she said. "And for my friend Argentina."

Tomé kept his eyes on the bottle in his hand. They softened a little. "*'Brigado.*" Dad helped Mom into the plane. "Come on, Keri." He touched her shoulder. "We're safe. It's over."

But it wasn't over for her. It couldn't be over. Not until she knew if God would answer her prayer for Dzumisana.

The airplane bumped along the short strip and dropped off the end before rising slowly above the surrounding hills. Just before they banked to the left, and her window was swallowed up in the blue of heaven, Keri caught a glimpse of the yellow plains of Mozambique beyond the edge of the green hills. She imagined she could see as far as the Indian Ocean glimmering in the distance, but she knew it wasn't so.

In no time, they passed over the crest of the mountains. The hills began to drop away and the high Zimbabwean plateau stretched out beyond them. Tea plantations and cultivated fields made patterns among the pasture lands. Black asphalt roads emerged from the hills and pointed like arrows to the small city of Mutare. Loaded trucks and passenger vehicles moved back and forth like worker ants along these roads. It all looked so normal, so African. *This is what Mozambique should look like. This is what it would look like if it weren't for the war.*

"Someday," something whispered deep inside her.

"God," she whispered back, "if you are who you say you are, then there is nothing I won't give for you. I'll go hungry or walk barefoot through the bush; I'll give away my medicine and my shoes. I'll come back to Mozambique when I'm grown up and help to make it happen. If you really are God, then there's nothing else that matters." A single tear rolled down her cheek. "If . . . " She wished she dared to believe.

The sun was still shining when Keri saw the tiny airport below them. It was bathed in shadow.

The pilot argued with the tower. "We're here now, aren't we? What do you want us to do? Fly to Harare and leave all those reporters and big shots down there?" He was a stocky young man in clean khaki shorts and a neatly pressed shirt with gold insignias on the shoulders. Looking at him made Keri realize how much she needed a bath.

She couldn't hear the tower's answer. Her father clasped her mother's hand. She knew they both were praying.

"What's wrong?" Kurt shouted over the roar of the engines. "Why won't they let us land? The sun hasn't set yet."

"The sun hasn't set *up here* yet," Mom explained, "but from the ground it's already gone below the horizon."

Kurt bit his lip. Keri didn't think she had the courage to ask God for anything more even if he was there. She would just have to wait and see what he decided to do.

"Let's put it this way," the pilot said into the microphone, "this plane doesn't have instruments to fly at night. I'm not licensed to fly at night. What do you think Harare is going to say when I show up there in the dark? Assuming my fuel lasts that long. Ask your supervisor what he suggests that I do."

He pulled the microphone away from his face and covered it with his hand. "They're discussing it," he said with a smirk at Dad. "Don't worry; we have plenty of fuel." There was a twinkle in his eye. "I think I convinced them that bending the rules this once was the lesser evil."

He held up his hand for silence while he listened into the headset. "Understand I am cleared for emergency landing on runway 2. I'm coming in. Over.

"We're cleared!" he announced.

Kurt let out a whoop.

They banked hard and circled low. The wing out Keri's window pointed directly at a cluster of people near the small terminal building. The lights in its windows showed bright in the quickly falling darkness. A fire truck waited at the end of the runway to race them to the other end.

"Standard procedure in an emergency," the pilot assured them.

The others grinned as though their faces would split open

as the plane landed and taxied to the terminal. Keri tried to join in, but her smile was weak. She hoped her father would think the tears in her eyes were from joy.

"Welcome to Zimbabwe!" a well-dressed African called almost before the door was opened. The pilot turned off the engine. In the quiet, the blood pounded in Keri's ears.

"Everyone all right?" An American woman in a neat blue blazer helped them down the little metal steps.

A pompous voice behind her announced that this was "an important day for the workings of diplomacy."

Keri shielded her eyes from the bright lights shining in her face. A television camera was aimed at her father as he shook the hand of the Zimbabwean official. Two Americans in business suits boisterously patted him on the back and spoke more to the camera than to him. The lights were so bright it was hard to see anything else.

"*Vovô!*" Kurt shouted beside her. "I knew you'd be all right!"

The elderly African emerged from beyond the cameraman. The boy leaped into his arms.

"Pastor Makusa?" Keri couldn't believe her eyes.

He laughed and tousled her head as he set Kurt down and shook Dad's hand. "I rested a day and a half in the bush," he explained. "On the second morning I thought if I had a stick I could support myself to walk, and when I opened my eyes I saw a stick nearby. I thought, if I had some fruit I could eat and regain my strength. I looked; there in front of me was a papaya tree with one ripe fruit. I took and ate. Supported by that stick and strengthened by

187

the papaya, I walked until I found a farmer who gave me a ride to the city. Your ambassador invited me to be here today."

"We prayed for you," Kurt said, gazing up into the old man's face.

"And I prayed for you," Pastor Makusa replied. He squeezed the boy's hand.

"*Vovô* . . . " Kurt looked at his father as though asking permission to tell. Dad was busy helping Mom onto a stretcher the Red Cross people had brought, but he smiled at Kurt and nodded. "Mfana is your grandson, Dzumisana. He didn't want to burn the house down. It was the bandits who made him do it. I gave him the ox because I thought you'd want him to have it, since he's really your grandson and not me. But can I be your grandson, too?"

Keri watched Pastor Makusa's face change from joy to pain to overwhelming love. "Of course, you can be my grandson." He hugged Kurt tightly, but he was shaking. His eyes were wet, and Keri knew he was longing to pull that other boy to him. There was a pain in her chest, and she could hardly breathe.

She was afraid to look around. If she searched the faces and didn't find the one she was looking for, she had to give up believing in God. If she didn't, there would always be the nagging thought that she was playing games and only pretending to believe. "A God who only loves some children isn't good enough," she whispered. She fussed over the blanket as they put Mom into the ambulance.

"It's OK, Keri," Mom said and squeezed her hand. But

Mom didn't know that it wasn't OK. The ambulance raced away through the gates at the side of the terminal.

"This way, please." The Red Cross woman led them out of the airport to a convoy of shiny black cars with little flags on the front. "The cars will take you to the hospital. You'll stay there tonight so everything can be checked out."

The cars pointed toward the lights of town. A driver in a crisp blue uniform smiled and opened a door for Keri. She hesitated. It was now or never. She ran her eyes hungrily over the crowd that was passing the gate and making its way to the cars. She held her breath, searching.

The diplomats got in the lead car. The reporters climbed into the last car, while the cameraman packed his equipment in the trunk. The Red Cross woman explained to Dad what would happen tomorrow. Kurt and Pastor Makusa stood close behind her. There were no ragged children, no young boys who had made their way over the mountains, no one else who had escaped the world of despair on the other side of the border.

That's it, she thought. *God doesn't care.* There was a cold hollow feeling in her stomach.

The driver motioned her toward the car. She took a long last look up the road, toward the Chimanimani Mountains over which they had come. The sky was still faintly gray, and the hills stood black against them.

A lone figure trudged down the road. It was a child; even in the dusk Keri could tell that much from his size. The boy's shoulders drooped as though he had come a long way, but there was an urgency in his step.

Keri's knees felt weak. The air seemed suddenly thin, and her lungs couldn't get enough. She took two steps toward him.

A pickup whizzed past the airport and climbed toward the hills. Its headlights lit the asphalt and flickered across the grass at the side of the road. They shone in the face of the walker.

"Mfana!" Kurt shouted. He started to run.

Dad hesitated with his hand on the car door. "Can you believe it?" he murmured. The cold feeling in her stomach washed away as warmth spilled over Keri like water in the bath.

"Dzumisana!" breathed the old man at her side. "Let us give praise!"

Keri wept.

> This is my Father's world.
> Oh, let me not forget
> That though the wrong
> Seems oft' so strong,
> God is the ruler yet.
> This is my Father's world
> The battle is not done.
> Jesus who died
> Shall be satisfied,
> And earth and heav'n be one.
>
> —Maltbie D. Babcock

AFTERWORD

The events of this story all happened to someone somewhere in Mozambique, southeast Africa, during their civil war of the 1980s. My husband and I lived in Maputo with our two children from 1985 until 1990. We traveled as a family to Chibuto by military convoy to distribute clothing to needy villagers.

Pastor Makusa's story is that of Pastor Raphael Manguela. In chapters 7 and 20, I use my translation of his own words dictated to his daughter, my dear friend Adelina Malombe.

Although Pastor Manguela does not have a missing grandson, Mfana's story has been repeated over and over in Angola, Liberia, Sudan, and other parts of Africa.

In 1986, seven missionaries were kidnapped by rebels from a farm near the Beira rail line. They were released three months later in Malawi. Although I corresponded with one of them to better understand their experience, this is a fictional story and does not reflect their view of events.

Mutare is a larger city than I have portrayed and has a lighted airfield, although there are many unlighted ones in the area.

Keri's spiritual struggle grows out of my own doubts and questions. The desperate situation made working in Mozambique feel like trying to fill a bathtub when no one had bothered to put in the plug. No matter how quickly you poured water, the tub would never be full, and if you stopped for an instant, it would soon be empty. I was emotionally drained and questioned whether God cared or even had the power to act. God graciously met me and answered my prayer.

The issues that provoked the war in Mozambique were complicated by Cold War politics, apartheid in neighboring South Africa, and the last struggles of colonialism. Each group claimed to represent the best interests of the people, but tribalism and greed played their part. In *The Wooden Ox* I have not tried to explain "the situation," as it was commonly called. I only seek to tell a story of people caught in the middle.

In 1992, the two major factions in Mozambique signed a peace accord. In 1993, democratic elections were held. The government party won and the former rebels became the main opposition party in parliament. The struggle to rebuild the country had begun.

LeAnne Hardy